Pack Saddles

&

Gunpowder

Susie Drougas

Susie Drougas

Pack Saddles & Gunpowder

ISBN-13: 978-1496058829

Layout and design by Katherine Ballasiotes Rowley
Cover Photo by Susie Drougas
www.SusieDrougas.com

Published in the United States of America

A piercing scream filled the mountain air freezing Dusty and Mike in their tracks. Spurring their horses into a full gallop, they headed straight for the trapper cabin at Sheep Lake. Dusty could only pray they weren't too late!

Set in the modern day mountains of Washington state, Dusty Rose and his sidekick, Mike Dracopoulos, ride and pack their horses in the high country. Living in Eagleclaw, a small town on the outskirts of Seattle, Dusty has a law practice and Mike is his private investigator. With a bad divorce under his belt, he feels like he's pretty much got life figured out—until meeting the beautiful Cassie Martin in a Seattle courtroom and then high up on a trail in the Cascade Mountains.

Cassie is a fiercely independent horsewoman and attorney. Dusty is drawn to her and isn't sure why, until their trails cross again in the middle of the Pasayten Wilderness. Cassie's quick thinking and courage come into play in a deadly confrontation and Dusty finds himself rethinking staying single all his life.

What starts out as a summer visit to his Uncle's outfit, turns into a life and death struggle for survival in the high country. The mountains are a jealous mistress and although many come to enjoy the bounty—all are not allowed to leave.

Arch
Rock

Ravens
Roost

PCT

Cougar
Valley

Tin
Shack

Crow
Lake

Elevator
Shaft

Crow Creek
Lake

Martinson
Camp

PCT

Crows
Nest

Little
Crow
Basin

Big Crow
Basin

Sand
Flats
Horse camp

Horse
Peaks

Dusty & Mike's
Basin Lake Camp

PCT

Crystal Mountain

and Ski Resort

Bluebell Pass

PCT

Dusty & Mike's
Crystal Mountain
Pack Trip

馬

CANADA

USA BORDER

Park Pass

Ross Family Camp

Ramon Lake

Sheep Lake

The Ashnola

Trail to Spanish Camp

Quartz Lake

Peevy Pass

Cassie & Terri's camp

Uncle Bob's outfit

Crow Lake

Mike & Dusty's camp

Corral Lake

Ginnie Forest Rangers camp

Whistler Pass

Pasayten Wilderness Pack Trip

To Billy Goat Trailhead

Acknowledgments

I want to thank my two beautiful daughters, Katie and Mikey, for their unwavering support and belief in me.

My Yak Writers group for their critiquing and inspiration.

My great friends that lent their time and talent to proofread and give me their opinion on this book.

April Laine Oostwal, a master wordsmith and current resident of Amsterdam, whose friendship and support exceeds time and geography.

And finally, my beautiful creative friend, Katherine Ballasiotes Rowley. Without her insight, encouragement and gift of graphic art, this book would not have been possible.

Pack Saddles

&

Gunpowder

Dedication

You know that big moment when life suddenly completely falls into place? You realize everything you ever wanted now was going to happen? Not only were you going to be able to ride and pack your horses, but you were going to have the best riding partner in the world go with you? Anywhere and everywhere? Yup, that's what happened…to me, when my Mike asked me to marry him.

This book is dedicated to my husband, Mike Drougas.

Prologue

Washington state has more than 13,000,000 acres of forested land. On the West side this is evidenced by the thick green trees and densely-wooded area as a result of the average annual rainfall of 53 inches. In the northwestern-most area the trees reach mammoth proportions in the Olympic National Park and surrounding forests. The Cascade Mountains divide the West side from the East side of the state. As you travel across the mountain pass, the salal and lush ferns give way to pine trees with grass and pine-needle laden forest floors.

The ownership of Washington's forest lands is divided into three groups: government owned, resulting in federal lands, national forests and parks; forest industry companies owned, such as Weyerhaeuser, Simpson, Hancock, Plum Creek, and Timber Resources, where access for certain activities is allowed; and individually owned by farmers and other private individuals, who may or may not grant access.

In total, Washington contains a huge area to pursue outdoor activities. There is skiing, mountain climbing, snowshoeing and snowmobiling in the wintertime. The summer opens a range from ORV (off-road vehicle) riding, horseback riding, backpacking, mountain biking, rock and mountain climbing, hiking, camping and more.

One sport, little known to the public at large, is packing horses into the mountains. Besides outfitters, there are still individuals who find the activity of packing their horses and riding in the mountains a fulfilling pursuit. The number of these people is small and it becomes smaller every year. Extreme pressure has been exerted by ecology groups to eradicate horses from the trails they trod carrying our forefathers to discover this great land.

In January of 1973 a small group of horsemen founded the first group of Back Country Horsemen in the Flathead Valley of Montana. Growth continued with additional chapters in Montana.

More states followed suit, and the Back Country Horsemen of America was born with a constitution drafted in 1985 and adopted in 1986. Today there are 23 states participating in BCHA with a membership of 13,300 and growing.

In 1977 in Washington state, Ken Wilcox founded an organization entitled Back Country Horsemen of Washington. The mission statement of BCHW, in part, is to keep public lands open for recreational stock use. This organization has blossomed into 34 chapters today in Washington and brought more than 3,000 people together, united in their desire to preserve access to the backcountry for horses and mules.

(Seattle, Washington)

Dusty hurriedly drove through downtown Seattle morning rush traffic. "This is just great, I'm going to be late to court," he thought. As luck would have it, a car pulled out in front of him right across from the King County Courthouse. He slammed on the brakes of his late model Ford Explorer and whipped into the vacated parking spot. Amidst horns honking and profanities, he jumped out of his car and ran across the street. A car took a sharp turn around the corner and slammed on its brakes with a loud screech, barely missing Dusty. "Another day in paradise," he sighed, walking in the door.

"All rise." The clerk stood, "Department 38 of King County Superior Court is now in session, the Honorable Mark Whitman, presiding." As the judge walked out in his black robe, Dusty arrived at counsel table. He quickly bent to set his briefcase down and stood up. Mike Dracoupolis, his private investigator, was standing next to him. "Thought you weren't coming, Boss," he said quietly out of the corner of his mouth.

"Please be seated. Glad you could make it today, Mr. Rose." The judge looked pointedly at Dusty.

"My pleasure, Your Honor," Dusty smiled amiably.

"Counsel, I see we are here this morning for a summary judgment motion. Mr. Rose, are you ready to proceed?"

"Yes, I am, Your Honor."

Dusty stood and walked over to stand in front of the bar. He smiled disarmingly at the clerk and court reporter. "Good morning."

Smiling indulgently the court replied, "Good morning, Mr. Rose."

Dusty was relaxed and as he warmed to his subject, he put his hand in his pocket. "Back in Eagleclaw we believe in progress. It's the thing that has brought our little town along to the point it's at today." Even though Dusty loathed progress, he was here today to argue his case...and win. "The Goldsby's Mill in its day was a stalwart of the Eagleclaw community, but times have been tough for all small businesses and the Goldsbys are no exception." Dusty walked over to his counsel table. Mike was sitting next to the corporate representative of Thorp International. Dusty took the photos Mike gave him and he handed up five color photographs to the clerk. "Your Honor, I would request that we mark these on behalf of the plaintiff."

The clerk handed up the photos to the judge. As the court reached for them he asked, "Has Ms. Martin seen these?"

"Your Honor, my investigator just got them to me last night."

"Ms. Martin, would you like to look at these pictures before I admit them?"

"Certainly, Your Honor."

As Cassie stepped up to the bar, she was furious. Of all the underhanded, rotten moves, bringing in evidence at the last minute so she had no time to prepare, she thought. As Dusty stepped aside, the clerk handed her the photos. Her heart sank. Unmistakably, the Goldsby's Mill. It showed a purulent yellowish material being pumped into the Green River. She looked down quickly at the date in the corner. Yesterday. No wonder they waited. They wanted to make sure she looked like a complete idiot. Her cheeks burned.

"Any objection, Counsel?"

"Yes, Your Honor. I am objecting to the timeliness of receiving these. I was not informed that Mr. Rose planned to take these pictures, let alone that he was going to present them today. This is the first time I've seen them. I had no time to prepare a rebuttal."

"Objection noted, Counsel. I will admit them," said the judge.

The clerk announced, "Plaintiff's Exhibits A through E marked and admitted."

Dusty continued, "Your Honor, as you can see from the

evidence, as recently as yesterday the defendants have still been unable to comply with current EPA regulations.

It's now time for Thorp International to pick up the gauntlet and streamline what's been started. Thorp has the financial ability to not only be fiscally responsible, but also conform to the latest Environmental Protection Agency standards. They will provide jobs for existing workers, and the proposed mill expansion will provide additional jobs for the people of Eagleclaw."

"Thank you, Your Honor." Dusty walked back to his chair and sat down.

"Thank you, Mr. Rose. Ms. Martin?" The judge looked at Cassie.

"Thank you, Your Honor."

The woman rose from counsel table gracefully. She had long brownish-blonde hair and she was blushing with determination. Cassie Martin. Dusty had never really looked at her before, but she was a beautiful woman. She stood tall and gracefully gesticulated to the court. He shook his head and listened.

Cassie felt like a manikin as she introduced her clients and her case to the court. Mr. and Mrs. Goldsby sat at counsel table, a couple in their sixties, with their eyes riveted on Cassie.

Dusty sat back in his chair, seemingly bored. It was really quite the opposite; he didn't miss a word. He jotted down a couple of notes as she spoke and handed them over to Mike, who looked and nodded.

"...the Goldsbys' community involvement and their reputation for hard work," Cassie continued, but the photographs stuck out like a sore thumb in her mind. It was difficult to concentrate. It felt as she argued like she had been physically struck. "This mill has been operating for generations in their family." Cassie outlined her case.

5

"In conclusion, Your Honor, my clients have made a good-faith effort to pay their debt. Contrary to Mr. Rose's photos, they have complied with all the current EPA regulations and a shipment of lumber is scheduled to arrive next week, which will enable them to bring the business out of foreclosure. I urge the court to dismiss this case, let my clients become solvent and get back to business."

"Thank you, Your Honor." Cassie sat back down next to her clients.

"Thank you, counsel," the court said as she sat down, and then went into its summation of the arguments of both sides. Cassie's clients sat up straight in their chairs. Their entire livelihood was at stake. She glanced over quickly at opposing counsel. Dusty sat easily in his chair next to his investigator. His impeccably cut navy blue suit worked well with his red and black striped tie and white shirt. He was handsome. Obviously really full of himself too, she thought.

"Counsel, I want to thank both of you this morning. You each did a great job and are excellent advocates for your clients." The judge went on to outline the facts of the case and then made his final ruling. "After reading all of your briefs and evaluating all of the evidence today, the court is ruling in favor of the plaintiff. You, of course, Ms. Martin are always welcome to appeal my ruling. Thank you." The judge got up and exited the courtroom.

"All rise," the clerk called. Mr. and Mrs. Goldsby started to rise, but suddenly Mr. Goldsby turned gray, clutched his chest and fell forward onto the table. "Wayne," came an anguished cry from Mrs. Goldsby. Cassie reached over to help, but Dusty and Mike had already picked him up and put him on the floor. "Call 911," yelled Dusty to the astonished clerk, as he hurriedly loosened Mr. Goldsby's tie. Everybody crowded around as Dusty began heart compressions on the inert man.

Within minutes the paramedics arrived in the courtroom. The judge came out of chambers hearing the ruckus and stood by as the paramedics hoisted Mr. Goldsby onto the stretcher and out the door. Mrs. Goldsby followed behind.

Cassie, feeling as if she had been poleaxed, gathered up her files from the table. She looked up and Dusty was standing in front of her. His deep blue eyes were filled with concern. "Cassie, I'm really sorry about your client," he said earnestly.

Mike came up behind him, "Is there anything I can do to help? Do you need help carrying anything?" Mike reached over to pick up her briefcase. She snatched it up, "That's okay. I've got it." She turned and left the courtroom.

"Really?" She thought, "Now they want to help?" She felt tears burning behind her eyelids as she hurried out the door. The more space she put between she and Dusty the better. "What an arrogant ass!"

Dusty stood for a moment watching her walk out and then turned back to his client.

The West

Circa 2014

Chapter One

As the city lights faded away behind him, Dusty felt his tension releasing as his shoulder and back muscles relaxed. Calmness descended upon him. It happened every time he did this drive. As he reflected on the contrast of the big city he had just left and the quiet serenity of the mountains around him, there was no doubt in his mind where he'd rather be. This Friday afternoon was a spectacular display of what the weather could do in the Pacific Northwest when it wasn't raining. The mountains were on fire with the late afternoon sun, and the sky melted into an azure blue, set off by bright peaks still topped with late July snow.

His truck pulled against the horse trailer as the road gained altitude and Dusty put it into four low. The Douglas fir trees were thick and green as they passed by. The trailhead was only 45 minutes away from his place in Eagleclaw. Dusty rested his arm in the open window of the truck. He felt the warmth of the summer air as it flowed in and filled his cab with the rich scent of fir.

He thought about his law practice. His dad and grandpa were lawyers. "Hell," he chuckled to himself, "it was a family tradition." A wry smile crossed his face. *If he would have told them what he really wanted to do: be a packer, they would have laughed him out of the room.*

Thank God for Uncle Bob. If Dusty hadn't been able to work in Bob's outfit packing in the high country when he was growing up, he hated to think of what would have happened. Living the summers high in the Pasayten Wilderness had kept him out of a lot of trouble. Too bad he had managed to find it later, he thought. When his marriage wasn't working, he should have known better than to think alcohol would fix it.

In the last ten years Seattle had become internationally popular with Bill Gates' success, and it was bursting at the seams with people and traffic. Dusty liked to think of himself as a small country lawyer. But in Eagleclaw these days that was getting harder to do.

What hadn't changed much were the mountains and forests, and that was where he was heading now. It was the best place to think—or not think. And with the emotionally charged courtroom he left yesterday, he would pick the latter today. Dusty's stomach tightened when he thought about the hearing in King County. Representing big corporations was never his bailiwick, but in the world of you eat what you kill, he knew he had to take the case. He couldn't afford not to; it was his livelihood. He hated that about his job. What was worse, he won the summary judgment for his client.

The idealistic woman attorney argued a very compelling case. Save the small businessman. He corrected himself; compelling in the emotional sense, which had absolutely nothing to do with the law. Cassie Martin represented the Goldsby's mill, a small family-owned mill struggling to keep its head above water. Dusty could understand why they picked Cassie; she was smart and she was talented in the practice of law. That much was obvious from her courtroom demeanor. His client, Thorp Brothers International, wanted to buy out her client's business and due to poor recordkeeping and out-of-date Environmental Protection Agency regulations, they put themselves in the path of foreclosure. It was a bitter victory. Watching the owner crumple on the floor and being taken out on a stretcher didn't really feel like winning to Dusty.

As the judge left the courtroom and the corporate representative slapped Dusty on the back, he looked across the room at the mill owner. His shoulders were slumped and he looked like he was folding into himself. An older woman next to him, his wife, rubbed his back. Then the man pitched forward grabbing his chest. Dusty and Mike had leapt into action, thinking of nothing but saving the man. Dusty felt his stomach go south again. *Damn it, why did life constantly twist him away from the person he really was? And why did he even allow it?* Scout, his Australian Shepherd, lay on the seat next to him. Sensing his owner's distress, nuzzled his hand. Dusty scratched Scout's head and felt better, "It's you and me, Buddy." Scout looked up, smiling, his tongue hanging out.

Dusty pulled into the Sand Flats Horse Camp just below the Crystal Mountain Ski Resort. The Back Country Horsemen of Washington built it, and he had helped. That was in the days before they had to make everything handicapped accessible. An old outhouse still stood in the middle of the camp; the door swung vacantly in the slight breeze. He sighed in relief. It was good to see that there were only a couple of rigs here. Sometimes the camping area was packed with mountain bikers. One side of the trail system was non-wilderness and the other side was designated wilderness. The mountain bikers usually favored the altitude and challenge on the non-wilderness side, but despite the threat of large fines, they didn't always stay there.

Dusty went into the large parking lot rather than a camping area. No reason to take any spots from the overnight campers; he wouldn't be staying around long. He opened up his pickup door and Scout bounded out of the cab. Dusty walked to the back of his trailer, opened the door and walked in to unload his two Appaloosas. "Well, come on out boys, time to do some work." He untied them and backed them out together.

As he threw his old Fred Hooks saddle on the black roan, the horse eyed him speculatively. "What's wrong, Muley?" The ruggedly-built horse stood over 16 hands tall with the old-style Appaloosa head that any Nez Perce Indian would have coveted. He radiated power and resembled a mule with his large head, except his ears were too short. Dusty straightened out his latigos and ran his hand under his horse's belly, checking for anything that might rub the cinch. Muley stood quietly, only his eyes intently following Dusty's movements. Although some people would find the big horse intimidating, Dusty knew better. Once he'd gotten past the impressive size and build with the intense stare, he saw the kindness and loyalty in Muley's eyes that nobody else saw. He and Muley shared a whole lot more than love of the mountains; they were both stubborn and neither one was built with give. If there was a mountain in front of them, by God, they'd climb it or die trying. *Guess it had to do with that winning thing again.* Dusty chuckled to himself and scratched Muley behind the ears affectionately. He was rewarded with a stony stare, the horse's highest form of affection.

After saddling his big roan horse, he turned to Cheyenne. Cheyenne was a tall, leopard Appaloosa, but not as stocky as Muley. He was broke late, after being a stallion for a number of years, but he was a calm, capable mountain horse. When Dusty threw the decker saddle on him, the horse didn't even flinch. He went and got his packs, already mantied, and put them on. As Dusty threw his crow hitch, a knot he used to tie off his load, he felt a warm feeling in the pit of his stomach. A part of him knew this was how it always was and how it always should be. He belonged here. Pulling his packhorse behind him and heading down the trail was always a *coming home* for him.

After getting his horses ready, Dusty tied his warm jacket and slicker onto his saddle and locked his truck as a couple more rigs pulled into the camping area. He easily swung into the saddle and pulled Cheyenne around behind him to start up the trail. Waving to the other rigs, he crossed the road and entered the woods on the side of the mountain.

Chapter Two

Looking up at the towering white peak of Mount Rainier and farther away in the distance Mount Adams, Dusty thought about all the places he could ride up here. They beckoned to him even after all these years. Few people knew about the backcountry that lay beyond the mountain peaks. As a boy, Dusty used to go to the ski resort at Crystal Mountain. He remembered sitting on the ski lift, looking up and seeing the snowcapped peaks. He had wondered, *What's up there?* Later, after having ridden up the Pacific Crest Trail and getting the postage-stamp view of the ski resort, things came much more into perspective for him. Dusty chuckled to himself. You never could take things at face value. There was always so much more to the picture. He knew that from the law, women, friends, but he learned it first up here in the high country.

The horses rhythmically ascended the trail, with the clinking of metal as a shoe struck a rock every so often. The mountain air mixed with the scent of fir trees made Dusty feel giddy and light-headed. It was intoxicating. It was the most intoxicated he got these days, having given up alcohol seven years ago. That was a good thing. If he had kept on with that, he surely wouldn't have been up here right now.

Back when he was drinking, his law practice had taken a severe beating. The fact that it survived was due to his father's and grandfather's good name. Thank God he got himself turned around. Now he had a nice little practice in a small town with Mrs. Phillips, his legal secretary, firmly at the helm. She insisted on being *Mrs. Phillips* and a *legal secretary* instead of legal assistant. She said that's what she signed on as 35 years ago, and she wasn't changing it now.

Dusty's mountain pack trips were his stress release. He often would saddle up and ride until dark, covering miles and miles of trail. Moderation wasn't something that Dusty was good at, so most people would not want to accompany him up here. The length of his rides could go eight hours, well past dusk. It all depended on how much he didn't want to think about on that trip. His horses were completely legged up. He rode them year round on the lower lying hills when winter made the mountains inaccessible and they were in excellent shape. The only thing that would stop his ride would be darkness and sometimes even that didn't stop him.

This time he only had a weekend, so he would just go the ten miles into Basin Lake for now. Winding to the top of the Norse Peak Trail the trees became smaller and more windblown. Scout kept his place directly behind Cheyenne's back feet, his tongue hanging out and happily panting along. A hawk screeched overhead as it circled in on prey, piercing the stillness. With the sun setting and the shadows starting to embrace the trees around him, Dusty zipped his Schaefer coat up as the temperature cooled.

As he began his descent into Big Crow Basin a small herd of elk on the far side of the bowl stopped and stared at him. He continued down the path as the elk went on—horses were of no concern to them. On foot one evening as he set out to get water from a stream, Dusty had walked right into a herd of elk. Seeing a man on two feet was a different thing altogether; they had bolted out of there at the sight of him. A man sitting on a horse and riding through the herd, the elk didn't bat an eye. Scout was a good trail dog and he held his ground following closely on the heels of Cheyenne, giving the elk only a speculative glance.

As Dusty rounded the bend near the bottom of Big Crow Basin,

Muley, Cheyenne, and Scout put their ears up. Dusty heard the sound of other hoofbeats. As he came out into the clearing at the bottom, he came face-to-face with a gray-bearded man in a weather-worn cowboy hat. He sat astride one mule and pulled another mule with a pack behind him.

"We-e-e-ll, look who we got here, Brighty!" Addressing his riding mule he proclaimed, "It's Dusty Rose, the lawyer feller!"

"And if it isn't Gold Dust Charlie! Hit the mother lode yet?"

"Well, Dusty, I have and I haven't, but I certainly cain't give away any trade secrets to yourself. Heck, if I did that, you might just leave your lawyerin' and start givin' me competition up in these here hills."

"Boy, don't tempt me."

Gold Dust Charlie was one of a handful of old-timers that spent a lot of time in the mountains. His trail name was Gold Dust Charlie and it stuck. His real name was Charlie Johnson. For generations his family had been coming up into the Crystal Mountain area. They had actually built a couple of cabins in the '50s, the Tin Shack and the Crow's Nest for an iron ore claim. The cabins were a Godsend to people lost in the wilderness or hit by a sudden snow storm. They were hidden and off the beaten path, but well known to those who frequented the high mountain trails of the Pacific Northwest. On a first-come, first-served basis, the cabins were open to whoever wanted to use them.

"On another subjeck, how is that uncle of yers doin' in the Pasaytens with his outfittin' business? I was thinkin' about maybe givin' him a look, see if he needed any help with his huntin' camp this fall. Me, Brighty and Boss are mighty partial to that wilderness country and it might give us a reason to get up that a way." Gold Dust smiled and turned his head, spitting out a stream of tobacco, careful not to get any in his long gray beard and moustache.

"Wow, Gold Dust, you're still chewing? Don't you know that's not PC!" Dusty grinned.

"Wall, I don't know about all that there PC folderol—but a feller has got to have one flaw anyway."

"I suppose you're right about that, flaws can be so hard to find; sometimes we just have to make one up ourselves!" Dusty's suntanned face split into a boyish grin, his white teeth showing under his thick brown moustache.

"Ya got that right, Boy. It's a tough one to do. Lucky fer me I got my chew," agreed Gold Dust, laughing.

Dusty checked his lead rope to make sure Cheyenne hadn't hung it up while standing still and looked back at Gold Dust. "I think Uncle Bob is always looking for help on his outfit in hunting season. It's hard to find good help to pack out fresh kill for the dudes. That's a big country, and he needs experienced men. It's way too far in to have a pack roll on you. And if you don't lose it all, you surely lose the time to get out, especially when you're rushing meat in before it spoils."

"Well, that's a fact. That's a fact. That's a great big country and I've a hankerin' to see it again before I'm gone. I'll have to give him a holler next time I'm in town. If you happen ta talk to him afore that, you might'n let him know I'm interested."

"I surely will. I know Uncle Bob would be happy to have you in his camp any time."

"Well, you have yourself a good ride. I'm headed down to the Crow's Nest for a few days and checkin' out things around there." The old man turned and spurred his mule down the trail.

"You have a good ride, too," Dusty called after him, then turned the opposite direction toward Basin Lake.

It never ceased to amaze Dusty what a small community of horse packers there were in the state. He had made a lot of friends doing trail work with the Back Country Horsemen of Washington. Dusty thought about the hard work of clearing trails of logs, rebuilding eroded areas, putting in water bars and check dams, pushing through slides, rebuilding or building bridges, putting back into this backcountry that he loved. It was almost as good as riding and he knew it was something he would always do. With the lack of funding the Forest Service wasn't able to provide the kind of trail maintenance needed to keep the trails open for the public. It relied a great deal on volunteer help.

Dusty dropped into Basin Lake, perfectly still except for a few small dips at the surface as the trout helped themselves to some early evening bugs. The sun rested on the surrounding peaks in a golden blaze as the day turned into dusk. Dusty scanned the large rock outcropping for mountain goats. He wasn't disappointed. High above, a small white animal moved around the rocks. He shook his head. How they stayed on those rocks was a mystery to him, but they always did.

Dusty set up camp quickly. A teepee-style tent went up with one pole and a few stakes. He put his Thermarest and down sleeping bag inside to fluff up. Then he grabbed his ax to gather wood for his campfire. In no time at all a good campfire roared.

The horses were out on their hobbles, having had their packs stripped. He put up the highline. He found a couple of trees that were spaced far enough apart to accommodate two horses, giving them room to move. He put on his tree savers, which were a seat-belt-like strap that encircles trees to prevent rope chafing. After slipping on the tree savers, he attached the highline rope to them and pulled it taut. The horses would be able to move around more and not have as much impact on the forest floor. Muley and Cheyenne didn't have their heads up yet and Dusty decided to give them a few more minutes to graze before tying them up for the night. It was always a good rule of thumb to wait until they stopped eating. It usually took about an hour. Any longer than that, they seemed to get into mischief. He'd learned the hard way he could spend a lot of time trying to track them down as they hopped out of the meadow on their hobbles; or picked a fight with one another.

Going back to camp, he opened a packet of dog food for Scout and pulled a steak out of his small cooler. His coffee pot had just reached a rolling boil so, since it was lake water, he timed it for seven minutes before throwing his coffee in. This was cowboy coffee. The coffee brewed in the water without a basket. He threw the coffee in, waited another 10 minutes, added a cup of cold water. It was ready to go.

Chapter Three

Dusty savored his flame-cooked steak, watching the sun slip from the grayish-black sky with stars just beginning to peak out above the mountaintops. The temperature dropped after the sun went down. He shivered, moved closer to the fire and finished eating.

As he drank his coffee and stared into the night, he heard hoofbeats in the distance. Scout perked his ears and issued a warning growl in the back of his throat. Dusty continued to watch in the direction of the sound. Within minutes an olive-skinned man wearing buckskins and moccasins rode into camp. Dusty took a drink of coffee.

"Whoa." The dark man pulled his horse to a stop and stared at Dusty silently.

A smile creased Dusty's face. "Well, Mike, you missed dinner. Highline's over there."

The darker man's somber face split into a smile, "Sorry, Boss, I got delayed. Mrs. Phillips seemed to have a lot of things for me to do that somehow you missed before you left."

Dusty sheepishly grinned. "Guess I was in a hurry to get cleared out for the weekend."

"No problem." Mike got off and dropped his packs in camp, then he took his horses over to the highline to unsaddle and hobble out for their dinner.

Mike was Dusty's private investigator. They had met years ago doing trail work by Mount Rainier. One thing had led to another and Mike had been working for him ever since.

Buckskinner was how Mike liked to dress. That basically came from his love of history. All of his clothes, saddles, implements and sometimes food, were period correct to 1826, the fur-trapper era. There were rendezvous for the "Mountain Men" buckskinners, but Mike preferred to keep to his own thing. He had told Dusty in the past, "When you think about it, the forest never changes. So if you have the same clothes, the same food and the same cooking utensils as the original mountain men, it's exactly as they had it. You are in your own time machine."

"I see you've given up on the cap and ball gun," Dusty observed as Mike walked back to the fire.

Pouring himself a cup of coffee, Mike grinned crookedly in the firelight. "I like that gun, it's just sometimes I really want to know it's going to shoot."

"Well, that's good, because I never wanted to see the thing blow up in your face, anyway. I really like my Ruger Vacquero myself."

"I know you do, Dusty," Mike took another drink of coffee, sat back and relaxed.

Dusty finished eating and tossed his steak bone to Scout, who happily began chewing on it. "I saw Gold Dust Charlie on my way in tonight. Said he was headed down to the Crows' Nest for a few days."

"Oh, yeah? I haven't seen him in a long time, what's he up to?"

"Same old thing, looking for gold. He did ask about Uncle Bob and his outfit, said he'd like to head up to the Pasayten to help out in hunting camp this year."

"That is a big wilderness. It's always a push to get meat out in time."

Dusty poured some coffee into his cup. "Yeah, that's why Uncle Bob needs all the qualified help he can get. Another interesting thing I just learned talking to the Mounted Border

Patrol at our last BCHW rendezvous in Ellensburg; they said that illegals coming in from Canada through the Pasayten are definitely on the rise. They're chasing them up there on horseback, but it's not an easy thing to do."

Mike thought a moment. "Geez, I think I would rather run into a Griz than an armed illegal. At least bears don't pack. Then when you throw in whatever contraband—or themselves, for that matter—that they are trying to bring into the states, the situation becomes pretty desperate."

"That's true. With so many cougars, bad weather, dangerous trails, now we have to worry about one more thing. I also heard that they were planning to reintroduce 15 pairs of wolves into the Cascade Mountains." Dusty took a drink of his coffee.

Mike snorted. "What's the matter? Don't they think they can walk fast enough on their own from Idaho?"

"Apparently not. That's okay. Now it will give the cougars a run for their money on the deer and elk we've got left."

"Or maybe some recreating Seattleites," suggested Mike.

"That too. Well, on that happy note, I think I'll turn in. I was planning a big ride tomorrow, 15, 20 miles. You interested?" Dusty tossed out the last of his coffee.

Looking up from the fire Mike said, "I'm always interested. See you in the morning." He reached for his bedroll to lay underneath the stars by the fire.

Dusty went into his tent and curled into his sleeping bag. Scout followed him in and took his place by Dusty's feet. The frogs croaked down by the lake and the night was otherwise silent.

Chapter Four

The Pasayten Wilderness

"Dad, Scotty, wait up!" Sally tried to adjust the backpack digging into her back. "We've been hiking for hours." She lifted her thick blonde mane off her back and wiped her sweaty forehead with a bandana.

"I told you this was big country when we talked about taking this trip, and you agreed that you were in shape and ready for the challenge." Her dad turned and pushed his wire-rimmed glasses up on his nose.

"Well, of course I thought I was in shape. What the heck. You work at Microsoft at a desk job, I totally thought I could keep up with you."

"Yes, but let us not forget, I run at least three days a week!" he shot back triumphantly.

"Oh, okay. Now I get it. I thought playing tennis on the school team was good enough, but apparently not." Puffing, Sally caught up to her waiting dad and brother.

"Well, don't worry, we're almost to the lake. Maybe another mile, if that." They set out again at a slightly slower pace, Scott now in the lead. A smaller version of his father; thin build, curly blonde hair, wire-rimmed glasses. Her 10 year old brother hiked silently and methodically down the trail.

Sally couldn't decide whether her feet hurt worse or her shoulders and back from the backpack digging into her skin. Even though they had left only a few days ago, it seemed like years since they had hiked out of Andrews Creek Trailhead into the Pasayten Wilderness. The trail had followed the creek and wound through thick trees for most of the way; the views were restricted and the scenery monotonous. After they arrived at Spanish Camp, that all changed. Sally was amazed. She felt like she had been in a dark closet for hours and the door just flew open. The woods fell away and they were treated to wide vistas with breathtaking mountain ranges and lush meadows. The late summer wildflowers were in full bloom. Indian paintbrush, lupine, yellow mountain daisies, along with smaller and more dainty flowers lining the hillsides.

Spanish Camp had a forest ranger cabin right at the trail junction, Sally, her father and brother posed in front of it for pictures. The cabin appeared well kept.

"Dad, I wish we could stay in there," she said, pointing to the cabin.

"Sally, it looks nice, but in reality we're much better off in our tent. Mice, other rodents and bugs enjoy the cabin too, and I'm sure you'd probably not want to sleep with them," Albert said in a reasonable voice.

"Ugh, I guess not." Sally backed a short distance away from the cabin as she looked at it appraisingly.

A single horseman pulling several packhorses passed by as they stood by the cabin. He waved and continued by at a good clip.

"That is an outfitter. He rides in and leaves drop camps for hikers. It saves them the wear and tear of carrying anything in but their light day packs. When they are ready to leave, the outfitter comes back in, picks up their belongings and packs them out. This allows people to access the backcountry who wouldn't otherwise be able to," finished Albert beaming.

Sally thought, *That would be the way to go.* In fact, even the horses looked pretty good. "Hey, dad, what about if we go with an outfitter next time to carry our stuff? Maybe we could even rent horses to ride, too," she added hopefully.

"Sally, you know that is just too hard on the horses. We are fit and healthy and it's just as easy for us to carry what we need in as it is for them to do it for us. It's not just the animals, it's the environment, too. We need to always think Earth First. "Let's have lunch here and then find a good spot to set up camp down the trail," suggested Albert.

Sally shrugged out of her pack and sat on the ground right in front of it. Pulling her lunch sack out of the side pocket she stared at the beautiful meadow in front of her. Her hand closed around her iPod in her pocket and she slipped the ear buds in. The music began and she relaxed.

"Sally Anne," roared Albert, "What are you doing?"

"Listening to music," she answered weakly.

"You're missing all the sounds of the wildlife. This is our time as a family enjoying nature together. You can listen to that stuff anytime. You're only 15 years old. It's your time to enjoy life," Albert added passionately.

"Okay, Dad, relax." Sally pulled out the earbuds and dejectedly replaced her iPod back into the backpack.

Two backpackers approached the cabin just as they were getting ready to leave. A man and a woman in their mid-20s who appeared very fit. "Hi."

"Hello," said Albert. "Where are you headed?"

The man stood with his feet a little ways apart, bracing his pack. The woman stood next to him, standing the same way. He took off his ballcap and wiped the sweat, "We're going to Lower Cathedral Lakes for a few days."

"That should be beautiful," offered Albert.

"That's what we've heard."

"I'm Albert Ross. These are my kids, Sally and Scott."

"Nice to meet you. I'm Nick King and this is my wife Katie."

"Good to meet you, too. Whereabouts are you from?" asked Albert.

"We're from Seattle," Nick answered.

"Well, small world, isn't it? We're from Redmond," Albert beamed.

"Yes, a small world and a short season in the beautiful high country," chimed in Katie.

"Speaking of short, we better keep going so we can find a camp by nightfall. Have a great trip," said Nick.

"You, too," said Albert enthusiastically.

The young couple headed back down the trail at a quick pace.

"See kids, the hills are full of great people."

"Yup, the hills are alive, all right," added Sally.

"Huh, I think I've heard that somewhere before."

"Me too, Dad," Scott said.

Their dad was born and raised in Seattle. He worked at Microsoft and his wife, Kathy was a CPA at Moss Adams. Although Albert and Kathy shared a passion for living green, Kathy was not a big athlete and preferred to keep the home fires burning and read a good book. So that left Albert to teach his kids about the great outdoors—which he did with a passion.

"Scotty, it's this lake over here on the left. We are home sweet home!" Dad happily announced. The lake sparkled in the late afternoon sun, quietly nestled in its mountain pocket. Sally whispered "Thank God," out of anyone's hearing. Scott and dad turned on the trail leading down to the lake while Sally limped along behind. It was late afternoon and they pitched their tent, inflated their pads and laid out their sleeping bags. As Sally helped her dad set up their kitchen area and gather wood, Scott went down to the lake with his fishing pole.

The lake was clear and shallow on the edges, dropping off abruptly after a few feet into a deep turquoise blue. Sally saw Scott climb up on a large rock and cast as far as he could into the middle of the lake, slowly reeling in his spinner. On his fourth or fifth cast his pole dipped and then came up. He let it happen again, but this time he pulled back quickly. After a short fight Scott pulled in a ten-inch Rainbow trout

"Son, nice job," said his father, walking down to the lake. "Looks like we'll be having fresh meat for dinner."

Scott beamed under his father's approval. He put his fish on his stringer and went back to try for another one.

"Now Scott, just one more. We don't want to deplete the resources for other animals."

Sally rolled her eyes and sat quietly on a rock watching her brother.

Other than at Spanish Camp today, they had not seen another soul for hours. The lake was breathtakingly beautiful, but at the same time it seemed arid and lonely. The mountain peaks stretched far into the north and faded to blue in the not-so-far distance of Canada. At times Sally wished her father would at least consider a gun. They had absolutely nothing to protect themselves.

As they sat around eating their fish dinner, Scott asked, "Hey, Dad, what's the name of this lake again. I forgot?"

"This is Ramon Lake. We are not that far from the Canadian border. Tomorrow we can do a day hike to Park Pass. It is loaded with different flowers and deep blue-green knee-high grass."

"Wow, Dad, you know a lot," Scott said admiringly.

"Son, it always pays to know your environment. In the backcountry it can even mean your life someday."

"Kind of a park then, Dad?" Sally threw in.

"Yes, you'll find the names are usually significant up here."

"Hey, Dad, what's a Ramon?" Scott asked.

"Well, Scott, to take a wild guess, I'm going to say this one is probably named after a person, not a plant."

"Oh." Scott said.

Scott looked sad. *Ever the little pleaser*, thought Sally. "Those were great fish, Scotty."

He smiled at her, immediately forgetting about Ramon Lake.

The fire crackled and the sky darkened. The mountain peaks around them stood silent like sentinels in the night. The half moon cast a whitish light on the hills and the stars sparkled. In the distance they heard a lonely howl.

Sally cringed. "What was that, Dad?" She glanced at Scott whose eyes were wide as saucers.

"Oh, that's just a wolf, probably howling at the moon. Don't worry, the wolves are our friends. It's actually very exciting to finally have them back again in their rightful territory. Canada was nice enough to give us some pairs, and they have been reproducing in Yellowstone Park for some time. There are packs in Idaho and most recently in Northeast Washington. So they're coming. Isn't that wonderful?" Her dad clasped his hands together, his grin lit up by the campfire.

Sally wasn't so sure how happy she was about the wolves coming back to their rightful territory, but at least it sounded like there was only one nearby. Scott yawned. Albert banked the fire, and they all went into the tent. Their third night on the trail, and so far Sally had not been able to sleep much on the trip. Every sound seemed amplified in the dark. She didn't know whether the sounds were there all the time and she couldn't hear them, or whether the animals just got louder at night. As the one wolf turned into a chorus of mournful howling, the hair on her neck stood straight up. Finally, at some point she drifted into a fitful sleep.

Chapter Five

Norse Peak Wilderness

Dusty smelled the campfire smoke and camp coffee before he even opened his eyes. The clank, clank of hobble chains, rip and munching noises let him know that Mike had already turned the horses loose to graze for their morning meal. The sun brightened the walls of his old canvas teepee tent, and Dusty relaxed into his warm bedroll. More comfortable here than his bed at the ranch. Scout ducked underneath the tent flap and out the door. Dusty stretched, got up, pulled on his faded jeans and green and black flannel shirt. He laced up his packer boots and went out to the fire.

The early morning sun was just breaking over the mountain rise and the lake was still. The morning air felt crisp in his lungs, like a cold drink of water. It was going to be a beautiful day.

"Morning, Mike." Dusty poured himself a cup of coffee from the big pot resting on the rock by the fire.

"Morning." Mike sipped his coffee and stared off at the huge protruding rock formation above the lake. "Where do you want to ride today?"

"Well, I was thinking about heading over to the Elevator Shaft, going over by Crow Lake, and coming back through Airplane Meadows. Maybe stop by and check on Gold Dust Charlie at the Crow's Nest."

"That's a good one. I haven't been through the Cougar Valley area for quite a while. Wonder if there's any cats over there," Mike mused.

"Yeah, I haven't either. I heard the Forest Service was talking to the Timberline Chapter about having a tri-chapter work party up there along the Pacific Crest Trail. I'd like to see what needs to be done."

The Timberline Chapter was one of the largest chapters of Back Country Horsemen of Washington. Their members were active in organizing work parties and working in conjunction with the Pierce County and Eagleclaw Chapters doing volunteer trail work for the Forest Service.

"As far as cats go, I guess we'll just need to be looking up and see what we see."

"Sounds good. The horses have been out for about an hour now, so we can saddle up in a little bit."

Both men sat quietly drinking their coffee, gazing into the fire. Scout looked intently in the direction of the trail leading into the lake basin. His ears perked up. The sound of horses' hooves faintly echoed in the mountain air, ringing off a rock every so often. Two horsemen appeared in the distance on the switchback trail coming into the lake. Small community as the backcountry riders were, Dusty knew he'd probably recognize one or both—and he did.

Cassie Martin, the lead rider, sat erect in her saddle on a beautiful gray Tennessee Walking Horse. Her hair, long and light brown, was loose under her grey Stetson. She was tall and slim beneath her tan leather chinks. Her fitted western brown leather jacket was visible even from a distance. A black and white Australian Shepherd trotted along behind her. The second rider was a small woman with long auburn-brown hair, following along behind on a brown and white paint.

Watching Cassie approach, Dusty felt a catch deep in his chest. He tried to ignore it. Something about a woman who carried herself with the confidence this woman did got to him in a way he could not explain. Seeing the valiant advocate for her client in the

30

courtroom paled in comparison to what he saw now. And he had to admit it, she was attractive. After what he'd been through with his divorce and his black days following, he was pretty sure he was through with feeling anything at all. But there it was…

Scout ran up to the horsewomen, barking at them as they rode into camp. The black and white Aussie met him partway.

"Heel, Sammy," Cassie said. The dog immediately dropped behind the gray horse and followed. Scout watched from a distance.

"Good morning, Dusty. Mike." The lead rider greeted them.

"Morning, Cassie," they replied.

"This is my friend, Terri." She pointed back to her riding partner.

Dusty and Mike both nodded and smiled at the second rider.

"Pretty creative on the summary judgment yesterday," Cassie said stiffly. "A little advance notice about the pictures would have been nice."

Dusty looked up at her, "I'm sorry, Cassie." He honestly meant it, too. She was a good advocate for her client, and she really believed her case should have gone to trial. Having lost completely with a dismissal on all counts was not an easy thing for any lawyer. "Is your client okay?"

Cassie looked down at Dusty. Her stomach still ached from his underhanded move yesterday. He looked directly at her and his eyes were a deep blue. It matched the high country sky. His teeth were very white, a contrast to his suntanned skin. *Damn, he was good-looking. And he looked like he actually cared. Remember, that's what lawyers are good at, courtroom acting.* She shook her head, *Fat chance that he cared.*

"He's going to recover. Thanks for your concern." Cassie thought of a lot of things she could say, but she held back. She hadn't had a chance to find out if her clients wanted to appeal the case yet and would rather not get in an adversarial position with Dusty if she had to deal further with him.

"Hey, Mike, maybe I could offer you a pay raise and you could come work for me."

Mike looked at her shyly not sure what she was meaning, "Well, I'll have to give that some thought," he said.

"Geez, no loyalty!" laughed Dusty.

The sun glinted off Cassie's Winchester rifle resting on the right side of her saddle in a scabbard. On the left side under her stirrup a saw rested in a smaller scabbard. Her slicker was tied on the back of her horse in anticipation of the unpredictable high mountain weather. This woman knew the backcountry, and she also knew the courtroom. Dusty petted her dog on the head as it came up to him and Scout hurried to his side, not to be outdone. It took a lot of grace to accept defeat as graciously as she did. It only added to the respect he already had for her.

"Where're you heading?" Dusty asked as he tossed the rest of his coffee out.

"We thought we'd head down the PCT, but we wanted to water first. Not a lot of opportunity up there." The PCT was also known as the Pacific Crest Trail. It ran from Canada to Mexico, running along the Cascade Mountains through Oregon and hooking up with the Sierra Nevada Mountains in California. In Washington, if there was a steep trail with severe drop-offs and challenging terrain, then it usually was the PCT.

Dusty nodded, impressed. Cassie and her friend were experienced riders or they wouldn't even be considering it.

"Well, we'd best be on it. Have a good ride." She pointed her horse to the lake and off they went, leaving Dusty and Mike to watch as the women watered their horses and headed out of the basin, the dog still trotting along behind Cassie's horse.

"Well, she's something, isn't she?" commented Mike.

"That's the truth. You sure don't see many like her."

For the people that rode the backcountry it was more than just a sport, it was a way of life. In town these people didn't dress any differently than anybody else. They weren't like the rodeo people with the big buckles and fancy western boots. Backcountry riders rode for the beauty and the solitude of the high country. The views and the challenges were intoxicating—its own kind of drug. In court they were lawyers, but out here they were horsemen, no different than the horsemen hundreds of years ago when the country was settled. That sense of timelessness and belonging were the core of Dusty's existence and a kinship of the backcountry riders.

Dusty and Mike saddled up and rode out, going the opposite direction the women had ridden. Scout followed along behind Dusty's packhorse, Cheyenne.

"You still planning on heading up to the Pasayten on Wednesday?" asked Mike as they switchbacked their way out of the basin, the peak of Mount Rainier growing larger over the top of the hill.

"You bet," said Dusty, leading the way on Muley. "I wanted to check in on Uncle Bob and then spend a few days up around there, by Cathedrals. Are you coming?"

"Well, I think so, if I can get the time off from my boss."

"I think we can probably get that arranged. Summer is a slow season for lawyering."

"Is it?"

"Well, it is in my office. Kind of works that way when you tell your clients you're going riding." Dusty laughed.

"Yup, I knew I picked the right office to work for." Mike smiled and drank in the view as Mount Rainier towered before him.

Chapter Six

"Everybody up and at 'em." Dad's voice sounded like an annoying chirping bird, thought Sally. "Hot water is boiling for the oatmeal."

She grimaced as she thought, *Yuck, that's worth getting up for?*

Her brother was just beginning to stir on the other side of the tent. She got up and dragged herself out to the fire. Another beautiful day. The only residual she felt of the isolation and dread from last night was the tiredness throughout her body. Mixing some Tang with the purified water, she sat by the small fire to wake up. As she listened to Dad's excitement about the day hike ahead, her mind drifted to absorb the vast hugeness of the country. The mountains towered into the distance as far as she could see. Changing from rock- and snow-covered peaks into lavender and indigo shadows, she truly understood now why people called the mountains blue. Somewhere on the horizon was a boundary where the United States stopped and Canada began.

Her dad bustled around laying out food on the log for their lunches and purifying more water for their bottles. "Let's get ready to go. It's going to be a long hike to Park Pass."

She and Scott grabbed their day packs and started loading up.

A few miles away in British Columbia, Canada, at Border Lake, the dilapidated blue Ford pickup rattled up the incline, pulling an ancient, shabby horse trailer behind it. At the end of the road, gears ground and the truck came to a stop. Two men got out. They unloaded three horses and tied them to the side of the trailer. The older man was in his late 50s, his face hardened by years of alcohol and too much time spent in prison. The other man was in his early 30s. He carried with him an air of sarcasm and lack of belief that life had much to offer except what he took.

"Hey, Clem, are you sure that's the United States?" the younger man asked with disbelief looking at the thick trees and meadows, "'cause it sure don't look the way I remember it." He lit a cigarette and looked expectantly at the other man.

"Well, they got the wilderness right there; that's probably why you don't remember it. Doubt you did a lot of hikin' either, did ya?" Clem gave a raspy laugh. "You cain't use motorized vehicles. Stupidest thing I ever heard of, if you ask me. Here, you brush the horses. I'll get the gear."

Tom moved his cigarette to the side of his mouth, grabbed a brush and curry comb and turned to the horses. Meeting Clem in prison had been a really great break for him; literally saved his life. Growing up, his mother was passed-out drunk most of the time. He endured his uncle's rape from the time he was 8 or 9 until Tom got big enough to fight him off in his teens. He thought back to that day; it was a real showdown, he laughed to himself. Tom broke his uncle's face and kicked him in the ribs. He couldn't stop. *If my friends hadn't shown up and pulled me off, I would have killed that piece of shit.*

Beating the crap out of his uncle had felt so good, Tom thought, as he attempted to brush the horses. They were thin, bones almost protruding through dull coats. Their feet were severely overgrown, hanging over their shoes. Giving into his personal rage had finally given Tom power. He could do whatever the hell he wanted. And the person who had let him down the most was his mother, *That bitch. And that's who was going to pay for it, but not her, the worthless slut.* It was little girls. He was empowered when he had his way with them, and that's what he did, starting with the neighbor who was no more than 7 when he invited her over for some candy. Tom laughed to himself at how stupid that little girl was and how much pleasure he got from doing whatever he wanted to her. It worked for him. Right up to the point they arrested him. They still never found the body. They had no reason to put him in prison. Once again, it was just because he was poor. *"Well, me and Clem ain't going ta stay poor, that's fer sure."* Tom's lips curved into a nasty smile.

"Hey, I thought you was gonna put shoes on these horses." Tom whined as he half-heartedly began brushing the first horse, a buckskin.

"Aww, I was gonna and then I thought, what the hell? Won't be that long of a trip for 'em. Why waste good nails?" Clem flashed a grin with broken yellow teeth.

"Well, that's just great. Real great. We don't know what we're packin, and now we don't know that we're gonna even make it."

"You jest don't worry about it," Clem snarled. "You do as you're told. Let me take care of the details." Clem had been taking care of the details for a long time. He was the mastermind behind their jailbreak and ultimate run to Canada. Tom was the perfect dimwit and so easy to manipulate, Clem patted himself on the back. He'd needed someone to help him smuggle contraband. He learned all about it in prison. Child molesters didn't have a great shelf life in the pen, so Clem covered Tom's back. He knew it would pay off in the long run. And *"'sides,"* he thought to himself, *"I ain't opposed to a little trim from time to time."* He smiled. *"Smart guys like me just don't get caught. Leastways not with girls"* He shook his head ruefully. He wasn't going to underestimate anyone ever again. The widow he was helping told him she didn't have any relatives. Grand larceny, indeed! Clem was just being a helpful handyman. Suddenly, out of nowhere, the nephew pops up with a property accounting. He snorted, *Never again.* He'd learned from his time inside, *"You jest don't get caught,"* Clem smiled exposing crooked yellow teeth.

"Yeah, whatever. Hey, I think these horses are brushed enough—I ain't no cowboy, you know. Let's jest get goin' and get it over with. I got a hot lady waitin' for me back in town when we're done." Tom leered, his cigarette still hanging in the corner of his mouth.

"Oh, yeah? Well, I hope this one's legal. You've gotten yourself in enough trouble, don'tcha think?"

"Oh, come on. Lighten up, would you? 'Sides, there ain't no such thing as too much trouble when it comes to women."

"Have it your way. Not my problem. Let's jest get this load done." Clem pulled the saddle blanket out of the trailer tack compartment.

As they finished putting on the packsaddle, Clem pulled a couple of pack boxes out of the back of the truck. "Tom, git over here and lend a hand, okay? This is pretty damn heavy for an old man."

"Be right there." Tom hurried over and grabbed the other end of the box. Together they loaded it on one side of the packhorse. As the horse stood unsteadily leaning to one side, they hurried back, got the other one and loaded it on the other side, balancing the load.

"Whew, that is heavy, I hope that ol' horse can make it," worried Tom. "Who the heck gave you this stuff to move?"

"I don't know. Some foreigner. He gave us plenty of money for it and said there was more comin' when we get ta the other side of the Pasayten. What do we care, anyway?" Clem beamed, proud of himself.

"We don't care, if the money's right. That's a fact," agreed Tom.

They finished putting on their riding saddles, filthy saddle bags and coats tied behind the saddles. Clem fitted his Remington .870 12-gauge shotgun in the scabbard to the right of his saddle horn. He adjusted a couple of ammo belts that crisscrossed his chest over his shoulders and put a .357 Smith & Wesson in a holster at his waist. He checked the little Derringer .22 strapped just above his ankle and readjusted the 10-inch bowie knife in the scabbard on his belt.

Tom had a high-powered 7 mm Remington rifle in his saddle scabbard and a 1911 Colt .45 semiautomatic gun in his holster on his belt. On his other side he carried a large hunting knife in a black case.

"Okay. Ready to go?" Clem asked.

"You bet. Lead out. The sooner we leave, the sooner we git done."

"Okay, then. The one thing we have to watch out for is the Americans have been getting a little persnickety about their border up here, so they got these mounted Border Patrols. Thing is, they can't keep them there every second—they only got so many men. So we sneak over as soon as they ride by. You got it?"

"You bet. I'm comin'."

The two men passed the small lake by the border and rode up the incline, carefully looking at all sides. Considering that it was illegal to carry handguns in Canada at all, they had more to look out for than just the American Border Patrol.

They topped the small rise and looked both ways. An approximate 50-foot swath cut through the trees, separating Canada from the United States. Every so often a silver monument stood, also marking the borders between the two countries. Off in the distance they could see a figure on horseback riding in the opposite direction.

"Hold up, Tom!" Clem ordered. He snatched up his binoculars and peered intently at the mounted figure in the distance. The green uniform of the mounted Border Patrol was obvious in his sights.

"Well, it's the patrol all right, but he is headed the other direction. Let's just let him get over that rise and then we head over and ride into those trees yonder real quick." Clem slid his binoculars back in their case.

"Okay. I'm right b'hind you."

The rider topped the far rise and disappeared from sight, and the two men spurred their horses and quickly galloped across the open area into the trees.

"Simple as that," said Clem, after they'd ridden for a while.

"Geez, maybe we're on to something here. Those foreigners might need more stuff brought over," Tom said, greedily thinking about how much money they could make.

"It's definitely somethin' to think on," Clem agreed.

Chapter Seven

Dusty and Mike headed out the trail to Crow Lake under another sunny, blue sky.

"You know, Dusty, for all the rain the Pacific Northwest puts out, when it's not raining it's just downright spectacular."

"Shhh, don't tell anybody. We've got enough people here now."

"Boy, that's for sure."

The snowcapped peaks gleamed in the sun, the creeks babbled with clear, clean water sliding over rocks and through grassy channels of sand. The clumps of lupine spaced along the trail perfumed the air with the sweet scent. Looking around him, Dusty found it hard to believe it could ever be any different up here in the high country. That was the deceptive thing about it. More than one case of hypothermia had occurred when people ventured into the high altitudes of the Pacific Northwest not properly prepared for the quixotic weather. Dusty always packed his slicker and energy bars—basically what he needed to comfortably spend the night if he needed to. You just never knew what could happen even on a summer day without a cloud in the sky.

Every winter Dusty told himself he'd had it with the rain. He was going to be like some of his "horse snowbird" friends; load up his living quarters RV and head down to Arizona with Muley and Cheyenne. Ride down there, maybe in the Superstitions or somewhere for the winter, then when the snow left he could head

40

back up here. The only fly in the ointment was what to do with his clients in the winter. He knew some attorneys who actually lived in Arizona, commuted by computer, and flew up when needed. That was a possibility, too. But darn it, he didn't want to work down there. He wanted to ride!

Riding horses was like a drug to him, an endorphin rush, and having done it long enough, he knew he was not alone in that. There was a whole backcountry population that felt the same way. He had spent a lot of time thinking and trying to figure out what exactly appealed so much to him about it. Lord knows, his ex-wife had made it such a point: *"Oh, going riding again?"* Like it was a dirty word. He had spent a good part of his young life defending his horses and his mountains, but why? Why was it so important that he had to leave the mother of his kids—or probably more accurately, she left him, but he didn't do a thing to stop her. It was the riding, the horses and the mountains.

The intoxicating air of the high country. The heart-filling views. The smoky smell of the campfire. The laughter of other backcountry riders sharing a story. The smell of horse sweat late in the day on a steep trail. It was all of that and more. Reincarnation wasn't a regular thought to Dusty, but he couldn't help but wonder about the change in himself once he got up here. It was as if he were back to himself. Hard to explain to anybody else, but nonetheless real to him.

They rode on, turning off the PCT and dropping into the Elevator Shaft. It was a user trail, unmarked or maintained on any Forest Service trail maps; Dusty and Mike's specialty. They cut downward through swampy meadows, intently looking for the blaze in the tree that would signify the start of the trail.

"Here it is," said Mike.

They hadn't spoken much to this point. Didn't need to. They had worked and ridden together so long they already knew where they were going. And they had an unspoken rule to never discuss work in the mountains.

This was a world separate and apart from any other they had left. The minute they got to the trailhead, loaded up and rode off, everything else stopped. In this world there were only the horses and the mountains. Their responsibilities changed. It was very simple: hobble your horse out in the morning, build a fire, eat, saddle up, and ride out. Come back at night, hobble your horse out, build a fire, eat, highline your horse. That's it. Dusty sometimes felt a pull so strong for that to be really the way things were, that he had to mentally pull himself out of his time warp so he didn't get lost in it

The two men descended the trail, which switched back and forth steeply and dropped altitude quickly. When they were almost to the bottom Dusty said, "Hey, Gold Dust Charlie said he was going to hole up in the Crow's Nest. You want to check and see if he's there?"

"Sure, why not? It's always good to see Gold Dust."

They cut over the hillside on the faint trail, crossing over old bridges not maintained but still intact, until they came upon the old log cabin with a tin roof butted up into the hillside. Smoke rose from the chimney and on the porch sat an old man, quietly whittling away on a stick. As they approached he looked up from his work.

"How's it going, Charlie?" The men greeted him.

"Hey there, fellers! Well, ye caught me in. Thought I'd do some catchin' up on my whittlin'. Been trying to make a chain fer I don't know how long. Some people it just comes easy to and t'others are like me."

"Well, gives you something to shoot for there," said Dusty.

"Yeah, that's fer sure." Gold Dust paused to spit off the side of the porch. "So where'n you fellers headed today?"

"Well, we're just going to drop on down and head over to Big Crow Lake. Heard they had some pretty good fish in there." Dusty pulled his hat off and ran his fingers through his hair.

"Yup, heard that too. All's you got t'do is be willin' to wade out through the swamp fer enough to get 'em." Gold Dust sliced his knife along the stick.

"I wanted to let you know that Mike and I will be heading up to the Pasayten next Wednesday for a couple week pack trip. I will be happy to let Uncle Bob know of your offer to help him in hunting camp." Dusty pushed his hat back on his head.

"Great. I'll give ya a holler in a couple of weeks and see if'n he needs me. The ridin's nice down here, but I've a real hankerin' for the big country again. It's a little crowded around here sometimes, 'specially with them mountain bikers."

"Isn't that the truth." Dusty nodded. "I was coming down Norse Peak trail the other day pulling Cheyenne and one of those things came up behind us real quiet. I practically had Cheyenne in my back pocket. They're not allowed up here in the wilderness, but that doesn't seem to stop them."

"That's a fact, but nothing that a few well-placed nails wouldn't take care of," Gold Dust Charlie said with a crafty look on his face.

"Amen," agreed Dusty. "Well, we better not keep those fish waiting!"

The old man went back to his whittling. Dusty and Mike turned and rode back down the trail, dropping quickly out of the woods and into the lush alpine meadow.

Chapter Eight

The town of Eagleclaw still managed to keep its small-town aura. Not an easy thing to do anymore with the rapidly encroaching sprawl of Seattle. Dusty's law office sat in an old storefront building, one of many on the block. Dusty parked his car and walked in the front door. The little bell tinkled when he stepped into the office. It used to drive him crazy, but now he rarely even heard it as the door opened and closed throughout the day.

His office was decorated in old western style. On the walls were western art, including his favorite, Charlie Russell. The furniture was leather, well worn. The metal art of a large packhorse led by a horse and rider crossing a creek decorated his coffee table. Issues of *Trail Rider* and *Western Horsemen* lay on the table, along with *Back Country Horsemen of Washington* and *Back Country Horsemen of America*.

His secretary, Mrs. Phillips, greeted him brightly as he walked in. "Good morning,
Mr. Dustin Rose!"
"Good morning, Mrs. Phillips."

Mrs. Phillips was kind of like the mountains, immovable in the way she thought and did things. There was the right way and the wrong way, and that was that. She had been in the office ever since Dusty could remember. When Dusty was fresh out of law school and started working in the office, it had been a little confusing with two Mr. Roses. Mrs. Phillips was not one to live in indecision; Dusty immediately became Mr. Rose, Junior. His mouth quirked in a rueful smile. Being a new lawyer was bad enough, but having *Junior* attached to his name was not tolerable to him. Trying to prove himself in an already overly competitive arena just simply did not lend itself to *Junior*. Also the fact was he was not a junior; his father was Radcliff Rose. So, Mrs. Phillips made a rare compromise: Dusty was Mr. Dustin Rose and his father, Mr. Rose.

The name stuck, even though his father had retired a few years back and was most of the time in parts unknown, be it Alaska in the summer and the Southwest in the winter. Dusty's full title remained at the law practice.

"Mr. Dustin Rose, your mail is on your desk. I shall bring your coffee in directly; it's just brewing now."

"Thank you, Mrs. Phillips."

Dusty walked into his office. Every morning she brought him coffee; she would not change that. She also looked at the fancy name of *paralegal* with disdain. She was and always would be his secretary. Made life pretty easy, actually, working in the law with no gray areas and having a secretary with no gray areas. If only life would follow the great example set by Mrs. Phillips.

He hadn't heard yet from Cassie, although he expected to, on the summary judgment he'd just won on Friday. Dusty thought for sure, after the emotional plea she had raised for her client and the complete dismissal, that she would quickly file a motion for reconsideration. Not that those worked—he had yet to see a trial court reconsider their ruling on a summary judgment. But it would make her feel better, and if nothing else, would lay the groundwork for her to file an appeal if her clients agreed. Hard saying what was next. Things in the law never were really cut and dried. If they were, he mused, he'd probably be out of a job.

He turned his thoughts to his day and began flipping through the interrogatories to prepare for the depositions he had scheduled at 3 p.m. Divorce cases were not his favorite. Too much emotion—someone could get hurt and he was really afraid it could be him. It had happened a few too many times in King County to make him feel comfortable in taking divorce cases. But as a small-town lawyer he pretty much took what came his way; refusing cases was not a good way to promote business.

At noon he grabbed his coat and called out, "Back after lunch."

Dusty walked to the diner, passing the shops lining Main Street. The local hardware store and a small branch of the Penney's store still remained, but the new Wal-Mart on the outskirts of town was taking a toll on the local economy. He walked into the Mountain Cafe, five doors down from his office.

"Well, good afternoon, Dusty." The heavyset woman with dyed red hair greeted him from behind the lunch counter.

"Good afternoon, Maude." He made his way to where Mike sat at the counter in the back with an empty seat next to him. As he greeted several of the other lunch regulars, out of the corner of his eye he caught the long light-brown hair of the woman seated alone at a booth.

Walking up to her table he stopped and faced her, "Well, hello again, Cassie."

"Hi, Dusty." Cassie sat with a file open, bearing no resemblance to the woman he passed on the trail the past weekend. She wore an Ann Taylor suit, impeccably dressed down to her Coach shoes.

"Business out in the boondocks again?" he inquired.

"Actually, yes. I am meeting with my clients here and you may perhaps be hearing from us again, or not, depending on how it goes."

"Yes, I wondered about that. Well, whatever way it turns out, it's always a pleasure to hear from you." As he glanced at her, once again, he couldn't help but wonder what kind of a woman she was, so at home in her business suit or out on the trail. Dusty sighed. *You sure don't see that very often.*

She leveled her light blue eyes on him, not giving away a thing.

46

"My clients do have a right to operate that mill; it's been in their family for years. If the big conglomerates keep shutting down the smaller companies, it's going to suffocate free enterprise."

"Yeah, I understand your argument." He flashed his white-toothed smile. It's just that I don't agree with it. And apparently the court doesn't, either."

Cassie blushed, the only giveaway to what she thought. "Well, we'll see." She turned back to her file.

"Yes, we will." Dusty ambled down the bar to Mike.

"Well, a bit of the mountains came down to our little restaurant, huh?"

"Yes, I guess so. And Cassie apparently isn't ready to let go of that case yet."

"Too bad," sympathized Mike.

"Yeah, it is. Of course, I couldn't have done it without you and your photographs."

"Don't remind me about that, it's just a job. It's pretty bad when we actually have to stoop to environmentalist issues to win a case."

"I know, I know, but the law is the law."

"Yeah, and the way the granola heads have the law cranked up around here, there is no way to run a mill at all without being in violation of polluting the water."

"Yeah, I don't even want to think about it."

Maude came up with the coffee pot. "Coffee?"

"You bet." He held out his cup.

"You want your Monday usual?"

"You got it."

"You too, Mike?"

Mike smiled. "Why not?"

Maude placed her pencil behind her ear and bustled off in the quickly filling restaurant to place the orders.

"You about ready to head out of town on Wednesday?" Dusty made a concerted effort not to let his eyes drift back towards Cassie.

"Yeah, I am. Not a lot to do really." Mike lived alone on a couple of acres just outside of Eagleclaw. He had two horses and that was it, so all he had to do was load up and leave.

Dusty was basically the same. It wasn't always the case when he had Sarah and the kids and the whole family thing, but that was long past. The kids had grown up and were in their 20s and Sarah lived in the city like she had always wanted. He remembered the black hole he fell into when it all blew up; alcohol, alcohol and more alcohol. After a family intervention, a stint in treatment, lots of AA meetings, and finally coming to the realization of what was really important in his life, Dusty was able to move forward. He knew his spiritual foundation in God kept him from his next drink and he knew for him God was in the mountains. That was Dusty's place of worship and his fellowship was with the other riders who were up there.

"Dusty!" Mike repeated, "Are you there?"
"Oh, sorry." He had been thinking too much again.
Mike asked, "How many horses are you bringing?"
"Oh, I'm just taking up Muley and Cheyenne. We don't need that much stuff. It's only a couple weeks."
The two men continued to discuss plans for their pack trip, oblivious to the scrutiny they received from the other table.

Cassie watched Dusty and Mike at the barstools through veiled eyes. She still stung from losing in court, but she wasn't going to give him the satisfaction of knowing it. Dusty was over 6 feet 2 and pretty hard to miss. Handsome in an outdoorsy rugged way, his packer boot rested on the iron footrest under the lunch counter. The mountains appeared to be etched into this man's soul, but the law was in his blood. It seemed to work that way in their profession, passed down from generation to generation. In her case, her father. He had practiced law in Tacoma for 42 years. A salty old retired Navy captain, the sea had never left him. They boated on the Puget Sound all her growing up years, the family as his crew. She was used to orders and the law as a young child.

The one mistake her father had made in raising her was issuing the family backpacks when she turned 12 and introducing them to the great outdoors in the Olympic Mountains. When the horses would go by with their riders, Cassie was captivated. From the time she first spotted them coming until they were walking out of sight, their shoes clicking on the rocks and their metal bits ringing, she knew she would get a horse one day and ride the mountains.

She tried to concentrate on the file on the table in front of her. The case seemed obvious to her, and why the judge refused to see it was beyond her. She had to somehow put it in a way that would make sense, which she had tried so hard to do last week at the summary judgment. The father and son owners of the mill had looked beaten before they had even walked into the courtroom. The ruling on the summary judgment had only reinforced their feelings of failure. She tried to reason herself out of it, but she felt that she, and not the system, had failed them. She rubbed her forehead as she leaned over the file. God, she hated that! There was nothing easy about the practice of law!

She scrubbed her fingers through her hair. She should be used to it. Nothing had been very easy in her house where she grew up. She had wanted a horse so badly, ever since she was five. When her father denied her, she went to the berry fields in Puyallup and picked berries through eighth and ninth grade. When she finally got the money together, her father allowed her to buy her first horse at age fourteen. She had to sell it to go to college and get a job. At 27 she bought another horse, knowing it was a way of life for her.

As luck would have it, by the time she got a horse and trailer, the Olympic Mountains were closed to stock on most of the trail systems, leaving only a couple of trails open. The actual trails she hiked and dreamed of riding on as an adult were now closed to horses by the environmentalists. She found out about the Back Country Horsemen in a Little Nickel ad and, after going to her first meeting in Port Orchard at a grange hall, she knew she was home. From there she learned everything she needed to know about riding her horse in the backcountry.

Cassie smiled, remembering when she and another woman entered Washington Backcountry Horsemen packing competition at their yearly rendezvous. They were the first women team in the state to enter the one-horse pack contest. Cassie and her packing partner Jan practiced and practiced with an older experienced packer at his ranch. They threw their double diamond hitch until they had it down. They loaded and unloaded their boxes until they got their weights right just by feel.

On the contest weekend, they trailered their horses over to the Ellensburg fairgrounds. The professional Forest Service packers from Nine Mile, Montana, with their huge string of mules were there. Smoke Elser, a professional outfitter from "The Bob," the Bob Marshall Wilderness, participated. He also was the author of the packer's bible, *Packing in on Horses and Mules*.

Cassie would never forget the adrenaline that pumped through her system as she threw her hitches, the crowd watching. They mounted up, Cassie pulling the packhorse and Jan following as they wound through the obstacle course. They passed the pig in a cage, a relative of the bear, and horses think it smells just as scary. Riding up the hill, remembering to hail the backpacker so he didn't spook the horses, they rode the course flawlessly.

When it was all over, the crowd gathered for the awards. When Jan and Cassie's names were called as the first place winners in the one-horse pack, the traditional all-men roster was stunned. Cassie felt like she walked on clouds. Winning that award felt better than passing the bar examination to her. It affirmed who she was. The law was hereditary. Packing horses and the mountains was finally coming into her own.

"More coffee?" Maude's voice broke the spell. Cassie blinked. "Uh, no thanks." She packed up her papers and left the restaurant.

Dusty watched her leave, feeling a sense of loss for some reason. He turned his attention back to Mike. "Yeah, I was thinking we could go in the Billy Goat Trailhead and see what Uncle Bob has going. He has that Dutch-oven cook working for him this season, and that guy can sing, too. Uncle Bob should be having some good campfires up there for the dudes."

"Wow, cooking and singing. You don't find that very often in one person." Mike smiled widely.

"Yeah, he really hit the jackpot with that guy."

Maude hurried up to the table with their sandwiches stacked on one arm and drinks in the other.

"Hey, Maude, I was just wondering, can you sing?" Dusty teased.

"Well, I have been known to belt out a pretty good shower tune now and then, but I guess in answer to that question: Not so's you'd really want to pay to hear it."

"Well, darn. I thought maybe if you could cook and sing, and possibly ride a horse…" suggested Dusty.

"Not on your life," she looked appalled, "even for a handsome guy like yourself. I am scared to death of horses." And off she went to pick up her next order.

Dusty laughed. "Guess you're right, they are scarce."

Chapter Nine

Sally followed her brother over the rise, and a huge beautiful meadow opened up before them. Filled with bluish-green waist-high grass and mountain flowers of all kinds, it was a riot of color and smelled wonderfully sweet.

"Is this it?"

"Yes, it is," answered her father.

"Wow." Scott stopped and looked around. "Dad, it's beautiful! Like a park for sure!"

"Yes, this is why they call it Park Pass."

Sally was finding out the Pasayten Wilderness was full of surprises; so many different kinds of beauty. Seeing places like this made the dark foreboding of the eerie wolf howls at night worth enduring.

Albert looked contently at the mountain ranges looming before them as he put canned chicken spread on his crackers. This trip had been just perfect so far; something he had always dreamed of doing with his kids. He was glad he had waited until they got old enough to handle it. He felt a warm sense of accomplishment to be able to take them into the backcountry. In this day and age people just didn't get the opportunity to have the experience and, for the most part, seemed to not even really know the wilderness still existed. The backcountry was a legacy his parents had given him and now he was giving his kids something very far removed from the hustle of the big city.

It was nice to be able to get back into the woods and not have to worry about the crime and stress of the city. There were wild animals, sure, but if you left them alone, they left you alone. Everyone knew that. He and Scott tied their food up in trees away from their camp at night, so that wasn't going to be a problem. The few people that they had met in the vast wilderness had been friendly, just like themselves, seeking a respite from the city life.

Albert watched Scott creep up on a brightly colored butterfly, just missing it as it fluttered away. Scott was a quiet boy and spent a lot of time by himself reading. This trip had been really good for him. Hiking into the Pasayten was an accomplishment for any adult, let alone a kid. Scott would have a lot to be proud of and share with his friends when he got home. Joining the Boy Scouts at such a young age had really paid off, for both Albert and Scott. He was amazed at the acuity his son possessed with the scouting program. And he wasn't the only one—Scott was promoted to the status of Boy Scout from Cub Scout at the young age of 10, a status very few boys were accorded. Albert had been able to share in the scouting days with his son, and now this great trip, where it all seemed to come together. Albert smiled widely.

"Hey, Dad?" Scott walked up.

"Yes, Son?" Albert jolted out of his thoughts back to the present.

"Tomorrow are we going to be able to go up to that lake you told me about, Cathedral Lake?"

"Sure. We'll have to break camp early and really move to do it, but we can." Albert smiled. *That will be another long one, but definitely worth the trip.*

Sally sat beside them. "Dad, why couldn't we have taken horses in here?"

"Now, Sally," her dad chided, "you know we talked about that before. Horses are too hard on the environment. We would lose all the opportunity to enjoy the outdoor experience by scaring the animals away before we got to see them. Plus horses raise all of that dust. And at the end of the day you end up taking care of them so much you miss the trip." He concluded, "You're much better off to be hiking."

Sally didn't appear to feel better off, but the horse argument was an old one. She had talked about wanting one ever since she was little, Albert had hoped she would outgrow it. Living in the suburbs of an ever-growing Seattle didn't leave a lot of room for horse pastures. Even horse rentals were moving farther and farther away. Seeing all this country had probably made her appreciate what the early pioneers must have gone through with their horses and wagons.

"Come on, kids, we've got a big hike back to camp. Let's eat our lunch," Albert said. They sat down and ate to the accompaniment of bees buzzing in the flowers and an occasional shrill call of a hawk diving overhead.

Sally followed her dad with her brother, Scott, leading the way down the trail. In spite of the warm sun on her back and the beautiful fragrance of the wildflowers around her, she still couldn't shake the apprehension of being so alone. The mountains and wilderness were vast around her. The snowcapped peaks enveloped them and at the same time stretched out into what seemed like forever into the distance. What if an animal appeared out of nowhere? Didn't they have cougars up here? Even grizzly bears? And what would her dad do anyway; politely ask it to step aside? She knew she shouldn't think like that, but as much as she loved the wilderness, Sally couldn't help but think of the danger that lay inside the beauty. Like the thorns of a rose. The nightmares she had been having at night and the wolves howling hadn't helped much with her sleeping.

Oh, well. Just a few more days and they'd be back in Seattle safe and sound. Sally smiled at that thought. She paused for a minute. Lifting her long blonde mane off her shoulders, she readjusted her headband. She hurried to catch up with her dad's quickly retreating back as they headed to camp.

Chapter Ten

Clem led the way as they came out of the trees and hooked onto a trail.

Tom followed along behind, his bony horse already breaking into a sweat.

"Which trailhead did you say they was meetin' us at ag'in?"

"It's by the Billy Goat Trailhead, a few day's ride from here," answered Clem, keeping his eye on the back of the Border Patrol agent as he rode out of sight.

"Good. Cain't wait to git the rest of the cash when we deliver it." Tom salivated at the thought of the money and what he would buy.

"That's the plan. We gotta call 'em when we git there." The horses walked along with only the methodical bouncing of the packsaddle as they went down the trail. In the lead, Clem pulled the packhorse, Tom rode behind. The trail was wide open with rolling hills and blue mountain peaks to the north as far as the eye could see.

"Man, they must have some money to be able to afford a satellite phone," said Tom.

"Yeah," agreed Clem, "But ask no questions and then you don't get no answers you don't need to hear. Let's just keep it real simple."

"Yeah." Tom lit a cigarette and threw the match down on the trail. "Simple."

They rode over a rise and looked down into Park Pass.

"Well, I'll be durned. Ain't that sweet?" Clem stared at the three hikers sitting in the meadow.

"Yeah, look at that sweet thang there, too." Tom sat up higher in his saddle, straining for a better look at the young girl.

"Let's go." Clem spurred his bony horse and pulled his packhorse down the switchbacks through the meadow toward the family.

Tom gave his horse a jab with his heels. "My pleasure!"

Sally heard the clicking of hooves first. She sat up and saw the three horses and two riders coming down the trail toward them. The horses looked sweaty, dirty, and beat up. Certainly not in good shape for what they were doing, but the two riders looked worse. The man in front was older, gray haired and sallow skinned. His ratty moustache drooped as he rode and his skinny arm pulled along the packhorse. Sally heard the rattle of the boxes long before the horses arrived.

Her skin prickled at something else. And then she saw the second rider leering at her with a look she hadn't seen before. Repugnance washed over her in a wave. The younger, heavier man had a cigarette hanging out of the corner of his mouth. His smile revealed missing front teeth. His face was pockmarked and the sweat stains ringed under his arms were now coated with dust.

"Afternoon," greeted the old skinny one as they came alongside the group.

"Good afternoon," replied her father. "Beautiful day to be out here, isn't it?"

"Sure is," agreed the second rider.

"Where're you folks staying at?" Sally felt the gap-toothed one's eyes lingering on her in a way that made her long for a shower.

Her dad, oblivious to anything but backwoods hospitality, warmed to the topic. "We came in Spanish Camp and we're staying at Ramon Lake tonight. We thought we might be taking in Cathedral Lake tomorrow."

The Old Skinny asked, "Upper or Lower?"

"Oh," answered dad, "Upper. Lower is quite the hike down into it and I don't think you really get much of a view from there. It's pretty thick with all the trees around it."

"Yeah, that's true, but I hear the fishin' is purty nice there," added Old Skinny.

"Well, we've had pretty good luck with the fishing at Ramon Lake," dad nodded proudly at Scott.

Scott flushed and looked at the ground.

"Well, is that a fact?" Old Skinny drawled slowly. "We may have to check that out." His mouth formed a sick smile at Scott.

Sally's skin crawled. She wanted these riders out of here as soon as possible. Sometimes her father's naivety seemed too much. There was definitely something wrong with these men; why couldn't her dad see it? They were also well armed. Each had a big gun hanging in a holster and a large hunting knife on their belts. Ammo was crisscrossed on Old Skinny. The way the second rider smirked at her made the hair rise on the back of her neck. Horses or no horses, they needed to leave!

"We'd best git. Nice to make yer acquaintance," Old Skinny said, the conversation coming to a halt.

"Likewise, I'm sure," dad replied.

"Come on Tom, let's get going," Old Skinny called back to Gap Tooth.

"Yeah, burnin' daylight." Gap Tooth threw down his cigarette and picked up his reins.

The scrawny old man in front poked a spur into the horse between a couple prominent ribs and they ambled down the trail, pack boxes keeping rhythm.

The second rider took one last leer at Sally, "Ma'am." He touched his beat-up, dirty cowboy hat and kicked his horse to a trot to catch up. In a couple of minutes, with a little puff of dust, they were gone. The only thing left was the cigarette smoldering in the dirt on the trail.

"Well, wasn't that nice," said her father. "It's good to know that at least there are a few other people up here in this big area, just in case we need any help."

"Help? Gosh, Dad," exclaimed Sally, "they would be the last people I would ask for help." She hopped up and stepped on the cigarette, crushing it out.

"Yeah, Dad." Scott for once had noticed something wrong, too. "They were pretty creepy. And they could cause a forest fire."

"Oh, now, kids," admonished Albert, "Everybody gets a little trail dust up here. That doesn't mean they're bad people. Anybody that enjoys the outdoors enough to come all the way to the Pasayten Wilderness can't be a bad person. Just wouldn't make sense!" He pulled out his water bottle and took a big drink. "We should be heading back to camp, though. It's going to take a while to hike back. And Scott, you may want to give fishing a try before dinner?"

"You bet, Dad," Scott agreed.

They picked up their day packs and headed back down the trail to Ramon Lake.

Sally couldn't shake the feeling of being watched. When she turned and looked behind her on the ridge above them, she saw the second rider topping a rise. It was hard to tell from where she walked, but she could swear he was still leering at her.

Chapter Eleven

Cassie drove home from her meeting with her clients. She felt an ache in the pit of her stomach. The law was black and white, but sometimes it seemed so unfair. She pounded the steering wheel. People were just trying to make a living. Her clients had been in business since the early 1900s. There was so much lip service to supporting the small businessman, but when it actually came down to it, it just wasn't happening.

As she pulled into her older farmhouse on close to five acres just outside of Black Diamond, her two horses raced up and down the fence alongside her car. It had been her grandmother's farm and she felt fortunate to have purchased it from her mother and sister. Development had built up around it over the years, but the thick green trees and the surrounding mountains gave the place a feeling of being much farther away.

She pulled up next to her Ford pickup still hooked up to the horse trailer. As she got out and headed towards the house, she was greeted by a high-pitched bark of her Aussie Sam.

"Take it easy, Sammy. I'll get your dinner in a minute," she told him.

He followed her to the front door and she let herself in.

She changed her clothes and went out to feed the dog and take care of her horses. As she came back in again, the phone rang.

"Cassie! Are you ready to go yet?" Her friend Terri was full of energy and excitement.

"Well, no, not yet. We aren't leaving until Friday, right?"

"Yes, I know, but it does take some prep time, and I have been getting all my stuff laid out! This is my first trip, you know!" Terri bubbled.

"Yeah, I know. The Pasayten Wilderness is the granddaddy of them all—at least in this state. I actually do have all my gear laid out and most of my food is ready. I put all the meat on dry ice except for our steaks for the first night in, and my canned goods and freeze-dried stuff is good to go."

"Yeah, me too! I already got my sleeping bag, tent, and all that stuff weighed and packed. I just can't wait! I've always wanted to go to the Pasayten; I've heard so much about it. How long did you say it would take to get to the trailhead at Billy Goat?"

"Oh, probably about seven hours pulling the trailer. We will head over North Cascades Pass, and it will drop us right in there," answered Cassie.

"Sounds good. I'll be ready at o-dark thirty." Terri's cheerful voice sang across the line.

"All right, then. Call me if you have any questions about gear. We don't want to repeat anything. We want to keep our weight as low as possible."

"Will do."

Cassie hung up. Terri's effervescent enthusiasm sparked her own excitement. It was great riding around the Cascades on weekends, but in the Pasayten you could spend weeks. She missed it a lot and couldn't wait to go back. She felt her heart race just thinking about it. The vast wilderness and challenges weren't for every horseman. The ride into base camp was between 18 and 20 miles. And once they got in there they still had to set up camp and take care of horses. Rest was a long ways off.

Cassie had lucked into meeting Terri on a ride with the Timberline Back Country Horsemen chapter. Every once in a while you met the kind of person with the determination to do what it takes to pack a horse into the backcountry. It was hard work and dangerous. A person had to understand their animal as well as the backcountry to be comfortable doing it. Horse wrecks didn't just happen to the amateur; there were a lot of things that could go wrong for even the most experienced packer.

As Cassie pulled a package of lettuce out of the refrigerator, she thought about one of the worst horse wrecks she had ever been in. It was many years ago, with her uncle, an experienced packer. She was 12 years old, and they were on a six-day trip into the Hells Canyon Seven Devils Wilderness. Idaho was known for its craggy, steep drop-offs, and that trail was no exception. Cassie enjoyed a gorgeous viewpoint of the impressive mountain in front of her and the blue spots of lakes below her. The Idaho Wilderness was a beautiful place. Her Uncle Jim sat on his riding horse and pulled two packhorses behind him, the one in the rear still pretty green. As they rounded a bend in the trail, a huge valley appeared before them, with a gigantic mountain at the end of it. The trail was very steep. The hillside actually cut back underneath them as they turned the corner, leaving them standing on a large rock outcropping. The trail continued, recognizable only as a narrow groove in the rocky hillside. Occasionally it would take a series of sharp switchbacks in descent.

Safely mounted on one of her uncle's seasoned horses, Cassie was looking around and enjoying the view. Suddenly, without warning, one of her uncle's packs began to slip. Cassie called out to him to stop. Before he could even get turned around to look, the pack on his first packhorse rolled, throwing the horse off the steep trail and dragging the second horse behind. The breakaway had not worked. The small rope holding the packhorses together had not broken; it held fast. The motion pulled the lead rope from her uncle's hand and not one, but both packhorses rolled down the steep incline, their packs unrolling and scattering the contents everywhere.

Cassie's uncle muttered a few choice words then said, "Here, hold my horse for me."

He jumped off the trail without hesitation and followed the wreckage down the hill. Both horses had stopped rolling and stood shaking. The packsaddle had rolled underneath the first packhorse. Jim slowly walked up to him, talking to him softly and freed him from the saddle and ropes. As he turned to go down to the second horse, the first horse decided to go back up the hill. It was a bad choice. Still too shaky from the fall, his legs gave out on him.

Cassie still remembered it like it was yesterday, the sick feeling in the pit of her stomach as she watched the horse roll down the hill right at her uncle. At the last second he seemed to step behind a tree, but it was hard to see what was happening with all the dust. The horse continued rolling past where her uncle stood and stopped just before a precipice, which dropped a few thousand feet to the canyon floor.

Everything halted for what seemed like minutes. She felt like she was watching a bad movie and her stomach clenched in fear. Cassie wasn't exactly sure what had happened to her uncle, but then he stepped out from behind the tree. The younger horse wouldn't let him near. He walked down to the older horse above the precipice and grabbed the lead rope. The horse calmly followed him back up to the trail and stood quietly while her uncle resaddled and repacked him.

The fact the horse would quietly stand and allow her uncle to replace the pack, which had almost caused his death moments before, struck Cassie in a way that stayed with her to this day. The trust these animals had in their humans was unwavering. She would always safeguard the welfare of her stock.

The younger horse finally picked his way up the hill and stood in his place behind the first horse on the trail. The whole process of repacking took a while since the manties had totally come undone and their gear was spread out over the steep hillside below them. Cassie was so overcome with gratitude seeing her uncle and horses unharmed, she barely noticed the gear strewn over the hillside.

Finding a friend to go along was not easy. Cassie found that plenty of men wanted to go with her, with the usual result: they were afraid of the horses or didn't want to get dirty. And she ended up doing most of the work. She wasn't into that anymore. It was her vacation and she wanted to spend it riding, not babysitting.

Terri turned out to be an able hand with a horse. She had two horses of her own and wasn't afraid to work with them. They'd already tried a small pack trip into McCall Basin earlier in the summer with great success. They had actually had the small meadow up there to themselves for once. None of the tree huggers had been running around complaining that the horses were ruining their wilderness experience. And the weather was beautiful. Cassie thought that was probably the first time that ever happened in her life. McCall Basin had its own weather system and when the sun was shining everywhere else, it was inevitably raining there. They'd hobbled the horses out in the meadow to graze, and then highlined them while they hiked up to the waterfalls. It was absolutely spectacular. While they were at the falls about 40 mountain goats actually trooped above the snowline, as if just to accent the beauty of the area. Cassie was filled with a sense of wonder every time she thought about the experience.

They completed that trip without one pack rolling or one animal mishap, which made the Pasayten trip that much more of a reality. Cassie checked out her gear again, making sure everything was in order. It wasn't hard to do. Next to her horse tack, her camping gear was kept in excellent order. She fondly picked up her kitchen bag, recounting the plates, cups, spoons and pots. She was really looking forward to the escape from her workaday existence into the real world of the backcountry.

Chapter Twelve

Sally's legs were tired and it was all she could do to put one foot in front of the other after the long hike from Park Pass. Even her dad had become uncharacteristically quiet. The sun sat low in the sky as they approached their tent and the lake was still as glass.

"Well, Scott, I'm not sure how good the fishing is going to be. The lake looks pretty placid out there," dad observed.

"That's fine with me," said Sally, "I'm not really in the mood for fish tonight, anyway. You can only have it so many times in a row."

"Now, Sally," rebuked her dad, "you have to be flexible to truly enjoy the whole backcountry life."

"I think I'll go down and give it a few casts, anyway," said Scott, giving Sally a dismissive look.

"Yes, Son. Better to have tried and failed than never to have tried at all."

"Oh, geez, Dad, how profound!" Sally rolled her eyes and headed for the tent.

The moon came up early, or so it seemed, that evening. With the light gleaming off the lake, the surface was perfectly blue, then black, reflecting the stars glistening above.

"Can you kids make out the Milky Way? How about the North Star? All you have to do is follow the far side of the cup of the Big Dipper straight up and you end up at the North Star, Polaris." Dad pointed towards the sky. "See it? It's that really bright star."

Sally and Scott followed his finger and saw a star larger and brighter than the others sparkling in the sky.

"Mariners have used that star for years for navigation. It points to the true north." Dad never passed up a teaching opportunity.

"Wow, that's cool, Dad!" Scott said. "They were telling us that in Boy Scouts!"

Sally thought, this was what dad had talked about when they planned the trip. He wanted to show them things they would never take time to learn in the city. She could tell by his smile that he felt it was a success.

Sally was mildly interested. She watched more to make her dad happy than really wanting to know.

"That's great, Dad. I think I'll turn in now." She felt tired from the long hike yesterday and today, then barely being able to sleep last night. The encounter with those disgusting men didn't help much. She shuddered. It was hard to get that second rider's leer out of her mind. It made her want to go wash it off. She went in the tent, lay down, and closed her eyes. The stillness was calming. Exhausted, she fell asleep.

Sally woke up in a panic. What was that noise? Her body tense, she listened again, barely breathing. There it was again. She heard a slight rustling on the side of the tent and something rubbed alongside it. The canvas was actually moving. Sally thought her heart would stop. The noise again. As the tent moved, *hmmm, hmmm, hmmm* emanated from the side, synchronizing with the movement of whatever or whoever rustled along the wall.

"Dad!" she finally croaked out.

"Whaaat?" Her dad mumbled, still half sleeping.

"There is something moving the tent!" she spat out.

He sat up and listened. The tent wall was silent for a minute, and then *hmmm, hmmm, hmmm,* quietly resumed as it moved along the wall.

"Oh." Her dad laughed. "That's a porcupine. He's just outside the tent. He won't do anything. Just don't hit the tent wall by him."

Sally was appalled. *A porcupine! As if I should've known that?*

She began to relax again, but not completely. She lay on one side and then turned onto the other, jolting awake as soon as she started to doze. It seemed like hours before she was able to drift off again. It was so alarming to be startled out of a sound sleep in a raw panic that it took her what seemed like hours to fall asleep again. Trying to get a decent rest out in the woods was a lot more difficult than hiking into it.

Chapter Thirteen

After passing the family in the meadow, Clem and Tom continued down the trail.

Tom chortled. "Clem, did you get a load of that sweet little gal?"

"Yes, I surely did," said Clem.

"Are you sure we gotta meet these guys right away? I wouldn't mind going back there and paying her a little visit," Tom wheedled.

"We get this delivered and you can pay all the little visits you want. But this here's bidness and bidness comes afore pleasure," Clem barked out.

Tom continued on behind Clem with a sullen look on his face. "I never was too good at bidness. Guess I must have spent too much time on the inside to learn much of it."

"Well, it ain't never too late to git good at bidness. And this here's yer big chance, so don't go screwing it up over no little girl," Clem reproved him.

The two men rode on, passing by meadows and through trees. As they crested a hill and looked down into Ramon Lake they saw the tent and the backpacker camp set up.

"Look, there's their camp. Boy, they must have hiked a fair piece today." Tom pointed at the tent by the lake.

"Yep, shore must have," said Clem. "Too bad we cain't stay and camp with them."

"And why cain't we?" demanded Tom.

"'Cause a you, that's why!" bellowed Clem. "You already been sent up once for rape. You just got out. Cain't you give it a rest for a while?"

"Sure, but who's gonna catch me up here?" whined Tom.

Clem considered it for a while.

"Well, it's not like she's all alone. Don't you think her daddy's gonna object some? He don't look like the type that would go fer a little sport," speculated Clem.

"Well, I guess he wouldn't be objecting if he couldn't." Tom gave an evil laugh.

"And that little boy, too?"

Tom stroked the whiskers on his chin. "Guess the same would be true for him, as well."

"I'm thinkin' that this is just getting way too big a deal for a little delivery trip. Maybe another time. Maybe on our return trip, or something. We gotta move on now,"

"They might be gone then," Tom pouted, disappointed that his newly found toy was being taken away so quickly.

"Well, I'm thinkin' it could be worse fer us if we were to let down our bidness people than if we was to stay and have some fun. So let's just move on. It's better to come back another day than be dead men."

"Well…mebbe," Tom reluctantly agreed.

The two men turned their string away from the lake and headed south down the trail.

Chapter Fourteen

Dusty's truck rumbled down the driveway, crowded on either side with salmonberry and blackberry bushes.

"I have got to get around to pruning those back," he told himself for the hundredth time. It seemed there were always better things to do. He had already gotten one notice from the county refuse department that if the branches weren't pruned, they were going to cut off his service. Scout jumped off the porch and ran to meet him, tail wagging. "Hey, boy!" Dusty reached down to scratch him behind the ears.

Every time he pulled in, he got the same peaceful feeling. The log house stood in a grassy clearing, surrounded on all sides by trees. The clearing was big enough to accommodate a picket fence and upper lawn around the house, a lower area with a big square lawn on the side yard. The porch ran along the front of the house and became a wide deck with French doors on the side. A rope swing hung from the large oak tree by the deck. Dusty left it there, just in case. Just in case of what he wasn't sure, but it needed to be there.

The front deck was crowded along the sides with rhododendrons, hydrangeas and small rose bushes, carefully planted years ago by his grandmother. Luckily they had enough seniority that they were able to be tended with just occasional watering in the summertime. The house itself was old. Dusty already had the logs underneath replaced from ants and termites eroding it, and he periodically had it sprayed. The cement caulking between the logs was a dead giveaway on the home's age. Not the best for the Pacific Northwest with all its moisture. Log cabin builders had long since switched to a more pliable putty that allowed the logs to contract and expand with the temperature. Keeping things basically the way his grandfather had was something that offered more peace to Dusty than tearing everything out and remodeling, so he left it the way it was.

It got pretty breezy in the winter without heat upstairs, another large bone of contention with his ex-wife. She wanted a place in town with wall-to-wall carpeting. The constant reminder of all she *sacrificed* got to be way too much. Dusty never felt life was about sacrifices for anybody, so he was glad to let her go for that reason alone. No matter how many divorces he did as a lawyer, he had yet to see a way through his own personal feelings of the shortcomings of a failed marriage. Even though they were now "friends" and everyone was much happier, there was always that black spot in his past of a marriage that didn't work and kids that had to go through the divorce with them. It had gotten better, but it was still there.

Dusty set his briefcase down on the red checked kitchen tablecloth and looked out the front window. Muley and Cheyenne were waiting expectantly in front of their troughs for dinner, their eyes glued on the cabin waiting for Dusty's reappearance. They gave him a low whinny of encouragement every few minutes to remind him to hurry up.

"All right, all right," he said. "Just let me change my clothes."

Chapter Fifteen

Dusty drove up to the grange hall on the outskirts of Eagleclaw and pulled into the parking lot. It was getting full and groups of people were gathered around outside of the building in the warm summer evening. He found Mike standing with a group of old-timers.

"Hey, Dusty," they greeted him.

Dusty smiled. "Well, if it's not the Over-the-Hill Gang!"

One of the old-timers corrected him, "That's the On-Top-of-the-Hill Gang, Dusty. We changed our name."

"Is that right?"

"We decided we never got to enjoy being on top and the next thing we knew, we were over it. So we just took it back," added Elmer, one of the elder statesmen.

The rest of the group all nodded. The men ranged from the youngest in their late 50s to Elmer at 84. They rode every week, rain or shine and went on a few campouts in the good weather.

"These guys know what they're doing," said Mike, standing by Eddie.

"Well, hey, I want to be in the On-Top-of-the-Hill Gang," said Dusty.

"Dusty, you're not quite there yet, but you just keep at it. You'll make it someday," said Elmer. Everyone laughed, including Dusty.

A call came from the grange: "It's 7 o'clock. Let's have a

meeting." The men made their way inside the building. Dusty dropped a dollar in the donations can and helped himself to coffee and a couple of cookies from the table near the entry.

As he walked over to the chairs, he was greeted by lots of smiles, especially from the single women in the chapter. He smiled back and then carefully averted his eyes, not wanting to offer any encouragement. He was pretty much a known quantity by now. The number of women riders greatly outnumbered the men and if you were looking, which he wasn't, it would not be difficult at all to find a date. Dusty enjoyed the companionship of the meetings and the work parties and potlucks. As for riding, he preferred to ride alone or with one or two horsemen—large group rides were for other people. He wanted to support the mission of Back Country Horsemen in keeping trails open for horses and mules, which was the main reason that he participated in BCHW.

"I want to welcome you to the August meeting of the Eagleclaw Trail Riders," a short man in a cowboy hat at the front of the room announced, and all the other cowboy hats turned to the speaker. He read the mission statement and the meeting began. The evening speaker was their own Tread Lightly person, Jane Steele, who urged the chapter members to "always clean up your manure at the trailheads and use tree savers with your highlines."

It was educational for new members and Dusty was always interested in the latest developments of Tread Lightly. Every year there were new ideas on how to be easy on the land. Although recently, Dusty felt they'd gone over the top with their pack-up-all-your-manure plan. He was pretty sure this was developed by the members who had one horse in a two horse trailer and stayed for only a couple of nights at the trailhead. Horses are proliferous grazers and it doesn't take long for them to fill up one side of a horse trailer with manure. Things would quickly get out of hand with two, three, or four horses in a four-horse trailer staying somewhere for a week. Dusty shook his head. Once again, it's the well-meaning trail riders trying to impose impossible regulations on traditional horsemen.

One of the latest threats to horsemen was the newly-minted microbiotic crust issue. The environmentalists had now decided that horses' feet stepping on the earth was destroying the earth's surface, irreparably. So the only solution was to severely limit where and when horse travel occurred. It would be truly laughable, except for the fact this had caused several trail closures and greatly limited the number and use of stock in areas that had been used since the first settlers arrived. Dusty thought about the Juniper Dunes area in Eastern Washington where riders were relegated to following one another down a single trail so as to not disturb the crust. One notch up from road riding in his opinion.

Another new restriction that just came out was weed-free feed. Hay growers were now growing hay certified to be weed free. Horsemen were required to feed the certified hay at the trailheads, and they must be able to prove it is weed free or a hefty fine would be imposed. It was even recommended that horses be fed weed-free forage for at least three days before going to the trailhead.

Dusty launched into a rebuttal speech in his head. For years horses had entered trailheads with no problem. Now invasive weeds were attributed to the horses, said to have been passed through their manure. The fact that scientific tests by Dr. Gower at the University of Wisconsin have proven that theory is false seemed to be of little consequence to the U.S. Forest Service. Certified weed-free hay was, of course, much more expensive than the noncertified and it was yet another burden that trail riders have to endure to ride the back country. Of course, the Department of Fish & Wildlife winter elk feeding stations didn't use weed-free feed, because they couldn't afford the cost difference.

It never ceased to amaze Dusty how the people thought—horses were okay to carry everybody out West—that never hurt a thing. But now with the advent of mountain bikers, hikers, climbers, and windmills, horses needed to be severely restricted in their use. The naturalists were imposing limits on one of the only truly natural things in the forest.

Dusty shook himself. He needed to just listen to the presentation. Getting all worked up about it wasn't going to change anything. His participation in Back Country Horsemen would help to some degree by keeping the horses' presence heard and seen in the backcountry.

Under old business they got to the Tri-Chapter work party. The president turned over the meeting to the coordinator, Val Norman, a retired plumber from Boeing. There were quite a few retired plumbers in the Eagleclaw Back Country Horsemen group, and a few of them had formed the majority of the On-Top-of-the-Hill Gang.

Val's job as the work party coordinator was to work with the Forest Service on trails that needed to be repaired. In the Pacific Northwest a lot of trail work was done on the Pacific Crest Trail in Washington. Val had been a member of the chapter for a number of years, was familiar with the trails, and participated in many work parties himself. He had a reputation in the chapter for riding hard and long, so while not everyone wanted to ride with him, they enjoyed his gung-ho attitude and wanted to help him out on the work parties. With the many budget cuts the Forest Service had undergone in recent years, the BCHW now held a prominent position for the large volume of volunteer hours they produced each year. Those volunteer hours were useful in getting work done clearing trails, building bridges, hauling planks and gravel into the wilderness. They also were invaluable to the Forest Service because they could use the hours in their grant proposals for funding other projects.

The work party was scheduled the last week of August at the Goat Hole at Crystal Mountain. Dusty shared the trail conditions he and Mike found from the previous weekend on their ride out of Sand Flats. A couple women volunteered to head up the cook tent again this year, featuring Dutch-oven cooking. They needed to get a head count for groceries. There would be a community tent for those who would ride in on their saddle horses. Riders would just need to lash on a sleeping bag and their essentials for the weekend.

Food and shelter would be provided. It was a great way to get work done while giving new people a chance to experience a night on the trail with the assistance of experienced packers. A benefit for both the Forest Service and the Back Country Horsemen.

One of the trail bosses gave a recap of last month's chapter ride. Trail bosses were appointed or voted positions within the Back Country Horsemen, people who had ridden the backcountry and participated in BCHW long enough to know what is required for the office. Someone recounted a funny story about the ride and everyone laughed. Plans were then discussed about the next chapter ride, which would be up at Ken Wilcox Horse Camp at Haney Meadows, located at Blewett Pass.

A young woman timidly raised her hand.

"Yes?" said the trail boss.

"This is going to be my first chapter ride and, well, I've heard things about the road into Haney Meadows. Is it difficult to drive with a camper and horse trailer?" she asked nervously.

A roar of laughter shook the rafters in the old grange. Haney Meadows had some of the most beautiful and accessible trails for experienced and inexperienced riders alike, with a road that was akin to crossing the gates of hell to get there.

The trail boss tried to keep a straight face. "Well, ma'am, I'm not quite sure how to put this. I guess the best way to say it is, it's a road with a bad reputation."

"How come?" the lady persisted.

"It is a consistent climb with a drop-off on one side and there's room for one vehicle at a time, at least one truck and trailer at a time. But there are turnouts periodically if you run into anybody," he added. "Best advice I could give you on that is to caravan with some other members. That way at least you won't have to be the ones to back up. Just check on the Eagleclaw Facebook page and see when a group might be leaving."

"Oh, okay." The woman sat down.

"Don't worry, Honey, you can follow me and my friends up," said an older lady in a straw cowboy hat sitting close to her. "It's not so bad. Least ways going up isn't so bad." She laughed.

The young woman looked encouraged and the president called for a motion to adjourn the meeting.

As Dusty and Mike walked out the door, Shelley McClain intercepted them. "Hey, cowboys!"

"Hey, Shelley," they said simultaneously.

"How come you boys are never at any of the chapter doings?" Shelley was known not to be shy and if she wanted to know something, she asked.

"Well, Shelley, you know that's just not true. We're going to be at the work party in just a couple of weeks," Dusty shuffled his feet uncomfortably. *Why haven't I ever figured out how to handle this stuff?* he asked himself.

"Dusty, that's not what I mean. How come you guys never come on any of the rides?" Shelley persisted.

"Just not into crowds, I guess," Mike broke into a big smile.

"That's another thing. Why does Mike always think this is so funny? I'm going to need to talk to him about that," resolved Dusty.

"Well, you don't have to stay with the group all the time." Shelley looked at Dusty meaningfully.

"We'll keep that in mind. Thanks for thinking about us." Dusty continued walking, eager to get out of there.

She pouted. "Okay, then. Just hoped you might make it sometime."

Dusty and Mike hurried out the door to their trucks.

"Time to head for the hills, Mike."

"I'll say, Boss. These meetings can be kinda scary." Mike opened the door of his truck.

"Yup, give me the cougars and bobcats any day of the week over some of these horsewomen."

The men jumped into their trucks and drove home in the warm night air.

Chapter Sixteen

Every time Sally started to relax she would hear something. A rustling outside, an animal cry, the tent flapping. Something. She must have been awakened at least four or five times during the night. When she finally fell into a fitful sleep, she heard her father's voice.

"Come on, kids, I got oatmeal ready! We've got to start our hike out this morning. We'll camp at Upper Cathedral tonight and then hit the trail to Spanish Camp the night after. You're going to love the Cathedrals. And your mom is going to be excited to see us!"

Scott obediently rolled out of his sleeping bag, grabbed his glasses and shoes and headed out the door.

Sally groaned and rolled over. *Finally get to sleep and it's time to get up.* "Be right there, Dad."

Her dad poured hot water in three bowls and stirred in the oatmeal. The lake in front of the camp was calm with an occasional trout jumping. The birds were singing in the early morning air. A hawk cried as it swooped overhead looking for its morning meal. A small fire crackled as they sat in front of it and ate their oatmeal.

"As soon as you get done we need to pack up and hit the trail," dad urged.

"Okay, Dad," Scott rinsed out his bowl and headed into the tent to pack his things.

"Sure, Dad," Sally added sleepily. The week up in the Pasayten had flown by, and she was ready to go home. She missed her friends and hanging out at the lake. It would be good to get back and catch up on everything.

It didn't take long to get the dishes washed and the camp packed up. They took one last look at Ramon Lake and headed down the trail. They had only gone about a mile when Sally felt the hair on the back of her neck stand straight up. *What now?* This didn't usually happen in the daytime.

They rounded the bend and in the middle of the trail stood Tom and Clem, their animals tied in the trees.

"Wa'll, look who we got here, Clem. It's the little family ag'in."

Dad, seeming oblivious to any danger, greeted the men. "Hello again. We're just on our way out. Beautiful morning for a hike," he exclaimed with a big grin.

"It is a beautiful mornin' for a hike, but I don't know about the goin' out part." Tom stood aggressively in the trail.

"Beg your pardon?" Dad looked truly confused by the last statement.

The men walked toward Albert, Scott and Sally. Tom reached out and grabbed Sally's wrist.

"We'll be takin' her with us," he said firmly and jerked her off her feet towards him.

"Now just a min—" her dad started to say, but never got to finish. Things moved at lightning speed. Clem punched him in the jaw in mid-sentence. Dad's pack weighed him down, after the blow to the face he went over backwards.

As Clem leaned in to finish him off, Scott jumped on Clem's back screaming, "Nooo! Dad!"

Meanwhile Tom dragged Sally off into the trees. She dug her heels into the dirt and tried to get away. She clawed at his hands, and he turned around and slapped her across the face. The blow knocked her temporarily senseless and she went limp. She came around again a couple minutes later and felt herself being dragged through the brush. Her arm felt like it was being pulled from the socket.

Tom drug her into a crude camp. A filthy tent sat pitched in front of a fire ring and a couple of pack boxes close by. A fire was still smoldering. The commotion had calmed down, and she could no longer hear her brother screaming.

Clem came through the trees. "I took care of 'em, Tom. They won't be bothering us no more."

Sally's stomach turned into a hard knot and she vomited.

"Dad! Scott!" she screamed.

Another blow caught her in the jaw. She saw a flash and then nothing. When she regained consciousness this time, Tom was standing over her.

"You'd best keep yer trap shut or you'll get more of the same, guaranteed."

Sally opened and closed her mouth, raw fear paralyzing her.

"We'll tie her up, do the delivery, and then head up to the Sheep Lake trapper's cabin fer a little fun," said Clem.

"Let's get to it then. I'm in the mood fer a little fun, and I don't know if I can wait that long for it." Tom's dirt-encrusted face broke into an ugly grin showing brown and missing front teeth.

Sally felt numb and sick.

Tom tied Sally's hands behind her back and one foot to a tree. The earthy stench of his proximity was causing her stomach to contract again.

"That will keep you here fer sure."

The men turned to their horses and began saddling. Sally slumped against the tree and watched, half closing her eyes and trying her best to be invisible.

Chapter Seventeen

Scott woke up. His right arm was twisted at an odd angle and he felt pain all over his body. He had been thrown off the trail and rolled quite a ways downward. A lone tree had saved him from plunging off the rock cliff not more than 20 feet below. He attempted to push himself up with his left arm. The pain shot through his body, but he was able to get into a sitting position.

"Dad?" he called tentatively. He didn't want to alert the men if they were still around. He saw a lot of trees and grass and rocks, but not his father. His pack had flown off his back in the downhill roll and was nowhere to be seen. It must have gone over the cliff. He pulled himself up on the tree and looked around.

All he could hear was the rushing of water from the creek. The bones in his arm were not poking through the skin, so thanks again to Boy Scouts' first-aid training, he knew he would be all right. At least for a while.

He needed to find his dad. He got up slowly and searched the hillside. Seeing a little patch of color just below the rocks, he began a painful crawl/walk down the side of the hill. When he finally reached it, it turned out to be his backpack. He opened it up and found an old T-shirt. He managed to rip it and tie up his arm. That helped with the pain. Scott dragged the pack into a little brushy area so it couldn't be easily seen, in case the men came back. He hiked along the creek, still keeping an eye on the hillside above him. The trees were thick and the sun filtering in now had almost a foreboding feeling, where before it had been a reassuring warmth in the shade.

After what seemed an eternity, although it was probably only a few minutes, he saw blue jeans and a T-shirt. Getting closer, he saw his dad lying in the fetal position against some rocks. Scott screamed, "Dad!" and ran over to him, putting his hand on his dad's arm. It felt cool to his touch. He felt his father's wrist and could detect no pulse. In panic Scott grabbed him and carefully rolled him over. The other side of his head was flat. The impact with the rocks had crushed the side of his head. Shock and disbelief washed over Scott. Death was not something he had ever encountered. Scott felt dazed. He ran his hand over his dad's bruised cheek. It felt cool to his touch. The skin was a deep purple and blood appeared to be coagulating in his good eye. The other eye was impossible to see from the massive head injury. Eyes burning and stomach clenching, Scott carefully laid his dad back down on the ground. Choking back sobs, he dug in the nearby pack and pulled a coat out. With trembling hands he gently placed it over his father.

"I'm going to go get help, Dad. I need to find Sally. Don't worry, I'll be back soon." Scott patted his dad's back reassuringly.

Scott crab-walked up the side of the treed slope, favoring his arm. He fought off the paralyzing shock that kept trying to stop him. Sobs welled up in his throat, and he pushed them back down again. He knew if he gave into crying, he may never be able to stop. For sure he wouldn't be able to keep going. Putting one foot in front of the other, he finally came back up to the trail. The good thing about being in front hiking was that he had seen the landmarks of the country as they went, so finding which way to go was not a problem. In his present state he knew it was going to take at least two days to get out. He hoped he would run into somebody sooner who could help him.

Scott saw the midmorning sun, but he didn't feel warm. He plodded robotically down the trail. The birds were singing. The creek bubbled off in the distance. It was as if nothing at all had happened. With each step the pain pounded in his arm, and worse than that, the void left by the absence of his dad and Sally hiking behind him was almost paralyzing. He had to keep his mind busy with other thoughts, even fantasizing that they were still back there waiting for him.

Scott hiked steadily for hours. He stopped for a few minutes to eat a granola bar, and then kept going. It was all he could do to keep his feet moving. His mind was exhausted from trying not to think about his dad and Sally. The pain from his arm was taking its toll on his strength. As the afternoon shadows grew long and the sun slipped down in the sky, he stopped to rest. Hiking at night was never a good idea, especially now with the increasing population of cougars, wolves and other nocturnal predators. Scott found a spot by a small creek and sat down. It ran back somewhat from the trail and he tried to decide whether he wanted to risk a fire. It would be great for the warmth and keeping away animals, but the fire also would be a big advertisement of where he was camping. After going back and forth with the idea, he decided to do without it.

Scott walked over to a group of heavily-branched fir trees nearby, their boughs touching the ground. He parted the branches and crawled into a little cave-like area next to the trunk with a thick blanket of fir needles on the ground. He lay down on his back with his arm resting on his stomach. He would just close his eyes for a little while.

Chapter Eighteen

It was still dark as Dusty pulled his four-horse trailer into Mike's driveway. Mike's two horses were tied to the hitchrail and his packs sat neatly on the ground next to it.

Standing next to his packs stood Mike, drinking a cup of coffee. Steam rose from his cup in the early morning air. "I wondered if you were going to make it."

"Yeah, I was trying to decide whether to go today or tomorrow, since it was so late and all" joked Dusty.

Both men would rather be in the mountains than anywhere else. Whenever they planned a trip it was an unwritten rule that whatever time they set up, they would arrive at least 15 minutes early.

Mike led his horses into the trailer while Dusty threw the pack boxes into the back of his pickup. Once they were inside, Mike put the fly masks on his horses' faces to help keep any foreign objects out of their eyes as they went down the freeway in the open stock trailer. He once had a horse blinded by a piece of dirt and never forgot from that point on to mask his horses.

Muley haughtily turned to look at him, his head held high and his eyes in their usual piercing gaze right through his fly mask.

"Don't you worry yourself, Muley. You and Cheyenne have plenty of room up there in the front. My horses are just borrowing a little bit of space in the back of your trailer," Mike assured him as he slid between his horses and out the back of the trailer. He slammed and locked the door, then walked around to the truck cab where Dusty sat idling the engine.

"Dusty, you have got about the most alpha horse I have ever seen. Are you sure he's not a stallion?"

"Yeah, I guess that's because he takes after his owner," said Dusty.

"Oh, yeah, I see that. In fact, that's what I always think to myself, *Man, that horse is just like his owner. What a stud!*" agreed Mike with mock sincerity.

The men had a good laugh. Dusty pulled out of the driveway into the dark, the sky just beginning to streak with dawn.

It was early morning by the time they passed Ross Lake on the East side of the mountains on the North Cascades Highway.

"Not too far now, Mike. You want to have breakfast in Winthrop?"

"That sounds like a plan. The restaurant ought to be open by the time we get there." Mike yawned and stretched, "After all, it's a tradition, isn't it?"

"Just wanted to make sure we hadn't made any changes."

"Well, as long as it's still Three Fingered Jack's, we haven't made any changes."

Dusty laughed. "As long as they've got the coffee on, anyway."

They pulled into the small, western-themed town. In the summer it became very crowded with tourists, making parking difficult. At this time of the morning, barely anyone was up and the streets were empty.

"Boy, this is some change from coming to the 'Ride to Rendezvous', isn't it?"

"I love '49ers Days, but the parade at the end gets to be pretty crowded," agreed Mike.

The Ride to Rendezvous was a four-day ride over Mother's Day weekend put on by the Washington State Guides and Outfitters

Association (WOGA) as a fundraiser. The riders and wagons covered approximately 100 miles in the week preceding the rendezvous. Entertainment was provided every evening along the way. The end of the ride culminated down the main street of Winthrop in a big parade. The different outfitters set up their camps in the little city park and ticket holders were able to come through for a huge meal on Saturday night, sampling the best dish from each outfitter. There was cowboy poetry, singing and entertainment provided by the members of WOGA in the evening on Saturday.

"Yeah, that's always a good time helping Uncle Bob out with his outfit that week," mused Dusty.

"You sure can't beat the food, either. I can't eat for a week after." Mike patted his stomach.

"Maybe I'll ask Uncle Bob if I can drive one of his wagons this year instead of being an outrider. That way I can eat more," Dusty said.

Mike laughed. "Good thinking."

Dusty pulled into town, turned right across the bridge and into the city park. A large red barn and a parking lot by the river held lots of open space for parking large rigs. They pulled into the almost vacant lot, got out and walked into town.

Chapter Nineteen

Sally lay in the darkness. Tom and Clem had come back sometime during the night. She had lost all track of time. The trauma and the pain had now been replaced by an anger and loathing that she was barely able to contain. She methodically worked at the ropes on her hands, and they were beginning to loosen. Her hands and legs felt paralyzed from being in the same position all night, but she knew it could be worse. Much worse. She needed to get out of here before anything else happened. These men had tried to kill her dad and brother. She could only pray they had not succeeded, but she was under no illusion. Whatever sick plans they had for her would only conclude with her death. She wasn't going down without a fight.

The horses stood still. One of the men's chainsaw-like snores broke the silence of the night. Sally moved her feet, trying to keep the feeling in them. She passed in and out of consciousness. The early morning sun was just breaking over the horizon when she awoke to the crackle of the fire. Clem was putting on the coffee pot.

"Come on out, Tom. We got us a big day t'day."
"I'll be out in a minute. Just git that coffee goin'."
Clem threw some more logs on the fire.

Tom came out of the grimy tent and picked up his cup. He cleared his throat, hacked a big wad of spit, and reached for the coffee pot. "Them foreigners seemed mighty glad to get their box last night, didn't they?"

"Yeah, they shore did. I love that we did so good they said they was gonna hook us up with another load." Clem reached in his pocket and made sure the large wad of bills was still there. "This is gittin' to be a mighty good job!"

"I'm likin' the fringe benefits myself." Tom looked over at the tree where Sally lay tied. "How did our little guest sleep last night?"

"Haven't heard a peep out of her," said Clem.

"Wall, that's a good thing. She's got ta save her strength," said Tom, and they laughed nastily.

Sally lay very still, pretending to be still sleeping. She had managed to almost get her hands free. The rope lay across them, still appearing tied.

Through half-closed eyes she tried to think. She wasn't that far away from the campfire and hot pot of coffee they had sitting next to it. An ax lay nearby against a tree, with a few thick logs next to it for the fire. She needed to think. Getting away was the only thing that mattered.

Tom and Clem talked for a few minutes more, and then Tom said, "Wall, I guess there's no more reason to stick with the formaltees. I think it's time to have a little fun. No reason t'wait for the Sheep Lake Cabin."

"I think you're right. You go ahead, but don't mess her up too bad for me." Clem emitted a raucous laugh and lit a cigarette.

Tom tossed the rest of his coffee into the fire and stood up. He walked over to Sally and grabbed her hands to untie her from the tree.

As Tom stood up Sally experienced a cold raw terror like she

87

had never felt in her life. But as he walked toward her, the fear changed to anger. A deep, feral anger. *How dare he think he can do this?* Tom grabbed for her hands to untie them from the tree. In one fluid motion, she slipped out of the ropes, stooped and grabbed a large piece of firewood.

"What in the hell…" exclaimed Tom, but before he could get the rest of the words out, Sally swung it with all her might and whacked him across the side of the head. He dropped hard onto the ground.

Clem was totally taken off guard, "Wall, I'll be damned. Looks like yer gonna need ta be taught a lesson here."

He threw down his cigarette and reached for his knife. Before he could get it drawn, Sally grabbed the coffee pot and threw the hot liquid across his face.

A bellow of pain pierced the forest silence as Clem staggered, grabbed his face, and nearly fell in the fire.

Sally didn't wait. She turned and ran through the woods as fast as her legs would take her. Whatever was out there was far better than where she was now. Sprinting through the forest for what seemed like hours, she had to jump over logs and streams and skirt around large clumps of vegetation. With everything that had happened she had become disoriented. Not knowing which direction to go, she did her best just to head in the opposite direction from which she had come. She finally found a thick clump of trees and brush and hid inside while she caught her breath. The sobs she had been holding back came in a rush. She laid her head against the sweet smell of the lupine and cried. Terrified for her life, all she could think was where was her brother…where was her father? She hoped to God they were alive.

Chapter Twenty

Billy Goat Trailhead

Dusty gave the cinch a final check and pulled his stirrup down. He grabbed Cheyenne's rope and mounted Muley in one fluid motion. Mike waited patiently, already mounted on his horse and holding his packhorse by the lead rope. It was midmorning and they were ready to ride.

"Come on, Scout, let's go." The dog bounded along behind Cheyenne, keeping an eye on Muley.

"How many miles you figure it is in there?" asked Mike.

"I'm thinking about 18. We can put our camp down at Corral Lake and see what is going on with Uncle Bob next door at Crow Lake. He uses that for one of his base camps. If we're lucky he might even be having some entertainment. He's got that Dutch-oven cook, that singing one I told you about—so I'd really like to check that out."

"That's probably a good plan. Too many more trips and you may be running out of clients. You may have to learn how to Dutch-oven cook."

"Well, if they're going to be that picky, then maybe they should find somebody else. I can only offer quality. I never said anything about quantity."

"Well, you know, that might be a winner. The way I hear it is nobody loves lawyers all that much, anyway. Maybe being scarce is the way to go!"

"I appreciate all your concern for me and my clients."

"Hey, what are friends for?"

"Gosh, I don't suppose it would have any effect on your employment, would it?" Pausing at a small creek Dusty let his horses drink.

Mike caught up. "Huh, wow, that never crossed my mind."

The men laughed. The horses finished drinking, and Dusty and Mike headed down the trail.

The rhythmic pounding of the horses' hooves, the smell of pine and fir trees and the earth newly freed from snow was a scent that Dusty could not remember anywhere else but the high country of the Pasayten Wilderness. The creeks were flowing at a pretty good rate and the trail had been cleared for travel only a week or two before they arrived. The freshly-cut log ends were next to the trail in several places. This year there was a lot of blowdown from the heavy winter snow. Dusty marveled at the fresh sawdust and so many trees, knowing that the Forest Service was only allowed to use crosscut saws in the wilderness. *That was a lot of elbow grease and strong backs*, he thought to himself.

The Forest Service men and women were pretty good with the crosscut saws. They could slice through some of the oldest and biggest trees just as smooth as slicing through butter. The crews were very fond of their crosscuts and even named them. Dusty knew that because back in Eagleclaw his Back Country Horsemen chapter had asked occasionally to borrow a crosscut for a chapter work party. The Forest Service was always eager to have help and happily provided some saws, but they were not the same ones as the crew had—they never let those go. Dusty understood that getting a good sharp edge was an art, and when someone had a sharp one he hung onto it. The duller saws were always the loaners.

He had bought a couple of crosscuts over the years. Packing those things in was something else. Before one trip, Dusty had bought a piece of old fire hose and sliced it lengthwise to cover the blade of the sharp saw. He then bowed it over the top of his packhorse, fastening down each end. That worked pretty well. Necessity was the mother of invention. As Dusty was busy patting himself on the back for that one, he rounded a corner and one of the ends came undone, causing a loud whap as the saw flew over the back of his packhorse, who was Apache at the time. She was fine with carrying the bowed crosscut, but the minute it started off on its own, Apache was done with it. She started bucking and that started the saw flapping even harder.

Dusty had bailed off his horse and, grabbing the lead rope, he did his best to calm her down fast. The biggest worry he had was her getting cut by the saw. Fortunately, that did not happen and Dusty was able to get her calm and get the saw off her back. It was time to rethink packing the crosscut.

No matter how many years a person packed, Dusty knew that horse wrecks happened. There was no 100 percent guarantee that a horse and load were going to do exactly what they were supposed to do, but there were definitely ways to give you a higher percentage of success.

He knew from experience the first thing was to get a mature, trailwise horse. The second thing would be to get the packs the right weight and balanced. It made all the difference in the world. Green horses on a pack trip can make things go bad in a hurry. Of course, green riders could do the same, so Dusty was picky about who he packed in with. Let Uncle Bob take the greenhorns in—life was too short. In the years that he and Mike had partnered up, stupid mistakes were no longer an issue.

The peaks rose on either side of them high above the tree line and the trail continued on its weaving path. As they came to another creek at a bend in the trail, they met a llama, a man and a woman with a handful of kids. The kids looked to be about nine or ten and Dusty was surprised to see them there—the length and difficulty of the trail usually weeded out the younger ones. He didn't think long about it, because as he crossed the creek Muley was looking particularly haughtily at the llama on the little bank just above them.

The llama was having none of Muley, either, and he was looking intently at the horse with an air of being ready to spring into action. Dusty shuddered to think what that action was going to be. The llama was fluffy with a black and white coat and had on an elaborate system of packs, which looked brand new. Dusty hadn't been around llamas a whole lot, but he'd heard when they didn't like something they could spit. He also heard it was pretty gross, like tobacco chew or something. Dusty was getting a little concerned he was going to find out exactly what they did spit. Muley was definitely giving the llama the hairy eyeball and his ears were flat against his head. Bad signs all the way around.

Scout had already bounded across the stream, keeping his distance from the possible scuffle, and he let out a little warning bark. Who it was directed to was unclear, but Dusty knew he was trying to neutralize the situation the best he could.

"Hey, how's it going?" Dusty called out to the llama handler. Sometimes it helped to get a little human interaction to remind the horses they are dealing with more than just a llama; that there's a person there, too.

"Pretty good," the man called back.

It didn't really seem to impact Muley at all. He had totally forgotten about the packhorse and was doing his best to get himself in position to either strike the llama or maybe even do a twist and let him have it with both hind legs. Dusty was countering each of his moves, and they were definitely having a disagreement on the next one.

Mike and his packhorse stood out of the way. He knew too well that when Muley was in his alpha mood, it was best to stay clear. Mike also knew that Dusty was an amazing rider. He kept a deep seat and he looked like he was actually enjoying himself. There was no doubt in Mike's mind who was going to win.

"Do you think it would be possible for you to maybe move your llama off the trail just a couple of feet?" asked Dusty. "Muley here seems to have his nose out of joint a little bit. I don't want him to get too close to your llama."

"Boy, no offense, Mister, but that horse looks like a black devil," the man said. Dusty could see he was very concerned about Muley's tirade and his llama's safety.

Mike could no longer stand it. He burst out laughing. "And that's on a good day."

Dusty took no offense. It certainly wasn't the first time he'd heard it. "Well, Muley does have his own distinct personality and he can take a little bit of getting used to, but once you get an understanding with him—why, he's the best horse I've ever had."

"He definitely looks like he's got a lot of strength. I will just take your word on the rest of it," the man agreed. He was stroking his pack animal in an effort to calm him down, but by the intent icy stare the llama leveled on Muley, Dusty doubted that it had much effect.

The man moved his llama and the kids far away from the trail and beckoned Dusty, Mike and pack stock on through.

"Thanks a lot. Have a great day!" Dusty called out.

"You, too," the llama man returned.

After they rode down the trail a few minutes, Mike said, "Well, the Mule Monster did it again."

"The Mule Monster? Is that a new one?"

"You bet," said Mike proudly, "The Earless Wonder."

"Okay. He may be earless occasionally, but let's see how he's doing at the end of the day."

"Well, you got me there. He does put the Energizer Bunny to shame, ears or not."

Chapter Twenty-One

The sun shown directly overhead and the trail stretched out before them. Dusty and Mike were silent in their thoughts and didn't run into anyone else on their ride into Corral Lake.

After riding miles on the thickly-wooded trail, they came to a valley and the trees disappeared. Dusty saw grassy meadows and rocky hills all around them. Looking north he saw the mountain peaks extending into the horizon until they turned a deep blue.

Dusty stared at the mountains as they rode along. "I just never get tired of this. It's just such big country."

"Yeah, I feel like I can breathe up here."

The trail switchbacked up a barren hill, and at the top the men looked down into a deep blue lake with a grassy meadow sweeping down to it on one side, trees behind that. The other side was lined with rocks and the foot of a mountain.

"Well, let's pick out a camp spot." Dusty led down the trail to the lake.

As they descended into the bowl they heard whinnying. Looking behind the lake in the trees, they could make out a highline with two horses on it.

Mike glanced at the camp. "Looks like we've got company."

"That's okay. There's plenty of room around here," said Dusty.

They went over to a copse of trees on the side of the hill a good distance from the lake. Stock were required to be at least 200 feet from the lakeshore, so this gave them plenty of room. The camp would be positioned on a hillside so they could look down on their stock grazing.

The men tied up to the trees and unloaded the packs off the horses. They stripped off the saddles, then made short work of hobbling the animals and turning them out to graze.

Dusty and Mike stacked their saddles over an old fallen tree nearby and looped the bridles over the saddle horns. Dusty threw a couple of manties over the top to prevent a squirrel, deer, or porcupine from chewing on the salty leather straps of the saddles.

They each set up their tents and laid out sleeping bags. Dusty set out some dog food for Scout. He lay down by his food and smiled appreciatively at Dusty.

"Well, that's just fine, Scout. You take your time and eat when you want. You've had a big day today for sure." Dusty chuckled and turned to set up the portable table for their kitchen area.

Mike used 18-gallon Rubbermaid boxes as liners in his panniers. Whenever they wanted to get into the boxes all they had to do was snap and unsnap the lids, instead of going through the whole process of buckling and unbuckling the panniers. And as long as they remembered to keep them shut tight, they were totally mouse proof.

"Now, last but not least, I'm going to set up the latrine." Dusty grabbed the shovel and the portable toilet.

"Boss, are you sure you have the training for that job?"

"Oh, yeah, I'm sure we covered it in law school. In fact, I'm sure it was on the LSAT, everything else you'd never need to know was." Dusty laughed as he headed down the trail away from camp.

A short while later he came back. "Well, I think you are really going to like this one."

"Oh, yeah?" Mike raised his eyebows. It was a running joke between them, Dusty's uncanny ability to place the latrine in the middle of the trail or some other public crossing. It usually happened when they got in after dark and what appeared to be a perfect spot at the time just wasn't the same in the light of day.

Mike followed Dusty out to the latrine site. It sat high on a rocky cliff with meadows and trees below.

"Well, you're right. This really gives the word *throne* a new meaning. But what the heck, at least there's no trails here."

"By the way, you have to check out my watering system." Mike clapped Dusty on the back and led the way back down the trail to the water just a little bit beyond camp. The stream was small and not flowing heavily; it would have taken a while to fill their buckets. Mike had placed one of his Rubbermaids under a ledge. Taking the hollow cylinder his fishing pole traveled in, he set that in the creek so the water flowed into the plastic box.

The second box was set just underneath the first box, allowing the overflowing water to pour into it and spill over the top back into the stream.

"The first box is our drinking water and the second box is our refrigerator. What do you think?"

"I think you missed your calling as a plumber and this is a first-rate setup," said Dusty, standing back in mock dismay. "Don't tell Val about this."

"Good point," agreed Mike.

"Let's get back and get to the steaks, what do you say?"

"Great idea. I'm hungry." They walked back to camp to build a fire and start dinner, Scout trotting along behind them.

Chapter Twenty-Two

Sally woke to a late afternoon sun piercing through the trees and the sound of voices. Lying flat on her stomach as close to the ground as she could, she carefully moved aside the bushes and looked out. The two men were standing a short distance away.

"Tom, what the hell were you thinking? Why did you let her go?" Clem snarled. His face was red and swollen, and he had a makeshift patch over one eye.

"That was the last thing I wanted to do, Clem," whined Tom. "In fact, I was never planning on letting her go."

"Well, we has got to find her now. No way we can let her get away from here. We'll have the law all over us and we's got more bidness to attend to." Clem fondled the knife on his belt. His voice dropped to a nasty whisper Sally could barely make out, "Let's get her."

"Wished we had us one of them tracker dogs."

"Well, we don't, but she cain't have got that far."

Sally didn't move as the men walked by. Her heart thudded in her chest. She felt light-headed. Fear was paralyzing her. She shook her head. She had made it this far and she couldn't give up now. She was going to have to get out of here. She waited for what seemed like hours. The forest was perfectly still. Bees buzzed over the alpine flowers. Everything seemed peaceful in the warm summer afternoon.

Sally did not want to move. Thinking about what could happen and what had already happened made her stiff with fear—she could not allow herself to think about it. Slowly she arose. Looking all around, she carefully and soundlessly moved out of the thicket of trees and brush. As Sally stepped out of her hiding place she took a couple of steps and stopped. All the trees looked the same. Sally had spent most of the time hiking behind her father and her brother. She mentally kicked herself for not paying more attention to the landmarks in the area. She took small steps trying to make as little noise as possible, straining to hear voices or any other noises that might give away the men's location. So far so good. She continued through the meadow taking cover in the trees as she went.

It was getting close to dusk and Sally finally felt like she was safe. There had been a couple of trails, but right now she was afraid to get on the beaten path. In a few more miles maybe it would be okay to try her luck on a trail, there was the possibility she could run into someone who could help her. Hunger started to gnaw at her stomach. It reminded her she hadn't eaten since yesterday. Sally didn't have any food with her; it had all been in her pack. A creek cut through the meadow grass. She squatted down, cupped her hands and drank. The water felt cold as it went down her throat. It helped to stop the gnawing hunger pains in her stomach. Even with no water purifier, any water was better than no water. Sally remembered from her Girl Scout days that swift running water carried less risk of Giardia than slow pooled water, so she took care to only drink from the middle of the creek.

Sally kept her eyes peeled for berries. She knew she had seen some on the trail because her dad and Scott had talked about it. It was a game for them. Scott would tell their dad what kind of berries they were and whether they were edible or not, and Dad would tell him whether he was right or wrong. Why hadn't she listened better to them? She was going to have to do the best she could. It seemed like huckleberries had come up a lot, so she looked for those.

It didn't take long before she came across a large area of bushes with bright red and purple berries. Their red colors shone through the leaves. These sure looked like huckleberries. Sally ate hungrily, they actually tasted pretty good. The berries were really small, though; it was going to take a lot of them.

She was so hungry and preoccupied with the eating, at first she didn't hear the crashing footsteps behind her. As she turned, she froze. Her breath caught. Standing rooted in place her eyes were riveted on the furry shape before her. A huge black bear stood on its hind legs, staring directly at her. Sally rose to her full height and for a long minute they stared at each other. She wanted to run in the worst way, but even if she wanted to, her legs wouldn't cooperate. The whole scene was surreal. Sally felt like she was watching from another place. The only thing she had ever heard about black bears was that they were totally unpredictable. Her thoughts raced. She had nothing to protect herself with.

The bear seemed to weigh the situation. He was staring at her and remained motionless for what seemed an eternity. Finally with a quick look at the berries and back at her, he dropped to all fours, turned, and bolted through the trees in the opposite direction.

Sally was unable to move for a while afterward. Her body felt weary and her mind was exhausted. She tried to focus, but she felt dazed and tired. With trembling hands, she plucked a few more handfuls of berries and then looked for someplace that would give her any amount of security in the middle of a million-acre forest with bears and two men who wanted her dead. It was going to be another really long night.

She stumbled through the bushes and pulled her shaking legs over the rocks on the hillside, panting. She found an area where a rock had split, with half lying over the top of the other, surrounded by more berry bushes. This would have to do. Sally lay on the ground and covered herself with leaves and dirt, trying to insulate herself the best she could against the dropping evening temperature. Mentally she kept running through the events of the day, praying that her dad and Scott were okay. She was exhausted. The worry and physical stress finally took its toll and she fell asleep.

Chapter Twenty-Three

Dusty and Mike sat with a cup of coffee in front of the crackling campfire after finishing their dinner. The temperature had dropped as the sun passed behind the surrounding mountain peaks, and the shadows grew long around them. It had been a long ride in and a really good day. The horses were highlined for the evening and everything was peaceful.

"Hello, the camp!" called out a cheerful voice. A short, medium-built woman in her early '40s with long hair walked into their camp. She had on a ranger outfit, but no pack or sidearm.

"Hello," the men returned.

"Would you like a cup of coffee?" asked Dusty.

A smile broke through on her tan face. "I'd love one! My name is Ginnie and I'm the backcountry ranger for this region of the Pasayten."

"I'm Dusty and this is Mike."

"So I see you just got in. What are your plans?" She sat down and made herself comfortable by the fire.

"Well, first off we were going to go over to Crow Lake and see if my Uncle Bob is there. He has an outfit up here," said Dusty.

"I can answer that for you. I just got back from Crow Lake myself, and yes, he is in there. He's got a group of dudes staying at his base camp and doing day rides out this week. He and his cook invited me over to dinner tomorrow night for Dutch-oven cooking and entertainment." She smiled, "It seems his cook is also pretty good with a guitar."

"So I've heard. We better pay them a visit tomorrow morning and see if we can't get an invite, too." Dusty picked up the coffee pot off the rock by the fire and poured some into a blue metal cup.

"Look out; the metal really picks up the heat," he cautioned, handing it to her by the cup part with the handle out.

"Much obliged. Hopefully my horses are still down there on the highline. I had them out to graze earlier this afternoon."

"Yes, we saw them when we rode in late this afternoon. You should be fine," Mike assured her.

"Are you two with any group or just by yourselves?"

"We're here alone," replied Dusty.

"We belong to the Back Country Horsemen, but we prefer to ride alone," Mike explained.

"Yes, I can understand that. I've been up here for most of the summer myself, so I welcome some company. I always enjoy your Uncle Bob's outfit when I'm down this way. Since the Forest Service has greatly cut back on wilderness rangers, I've got a really big area to cover. One other ranger and I have the whole Pasayten Wilderness and the Sawtooths as well."

"Boy, that's a lot of country. Wish we could help you," said Dusty.

Ginnie crossed her legs and sat back. "Well, that's something I have given some thought to, I could use some help. I would need experienced horse packers. If you guys could ride some areas and let me know what's going on, that would be great."

"That sounds like it's right up our alley," said Mike.

"I've had some issues this season with people holing up in their camps with lots of alcohol and guns. Don't get me wrong. I totally support guns. Of course, I can't carry one myself since I'm an employee of the Forest Service, but alcohol, guns, and belligerence is always a bad combination." Ginnie took a drink of her coffee and let that thought settle in.

"Yeah, that's exactly why I try to stay away from criminal law myself. Unfortunately, out in Eagleclaw we still run into the alcohol and firearm situation. Belligerence is kind of a universal problem," Dusty shook his head in disgust.

"Seems pretty chronic when you're trying to drive through downtown Seattle," said Mike.

Ginnie wrinkled her nose. "Yeah, I try to stay away from that place. We've also had some situations with border crossings, too. We do have the mounted horse patrol up there and drones flying over, but it's still really porous. It would do you good to keep an eye out for anybody suspicious. Times have changed a lot over the years," she stared into the fire sadly. "Maybe the Back Country Horsemen would be a group that could provide those kind of riders for me? I don't want them to do anything other than just report the location and situation to me. The Forest Service can take care of it."

"That's a possibility," said Dusty. "I'd be happy to bring it up at the next meeting and see if there are any takers. I could also get ahold of the state president and see if he can put it out to the other chapters."

Dusty, Mike and Ginnie visited about where they had come from and what their riding plans were for the week. The fire grew smaller and the coals were bright red.

"Well, I'd better get back to my camp and check on my horses. Thank you very much for your hospitality."

"And thank you for filling us in on what's going on in the area." Dusty stood.

Ginnie sat her coffee cup down, turned, and trudged off through the dark. She apparently didn't need a flashlight.

Mike yawned. "Well, it's been a long day. I believe I'll turn in."

"Yup, I'm right with you on that. See you in the morning."

Dusty sat by the fire finishing his coffee. He stared out at the still peaks surrounded by stars. Small star jewels twinkled in the huge black backdrop of the sky, illuminated clearly in the clean mountain air. He studied the Big Dipper and the North Star. Every once in a while he'd see a flash and trail of a falling star. He sighed contentedly. He had a good life. How many guys could come up here and really appreciate the mountains?

He set his coffee cup down and stared into the fire. Scout lay next to him with his eyes shut. Finally, after he found himself nodding off, Dusty stood up and banked the fire for the night.

"Well, come on, boy. Time to turn in." He turned and walked to his tent. Scout scrambled up and followed.

Chapter Twenty-Four

Scott opened his eyes and blew out a visible breath in the chilly mountain dawn. The trees above him were a thick canopy. In a couple of spots he could see through to the tall mountain peaks around him. The sun hit the snow on top of them in a bright orange-red. Then the urgency of his situation hit him. A sick feeling lay in the pit of his stomach. Dad. Sally. He needed to get help.

Scott sat up and rubbed his eyes. He opened his water bottle and drank what little water was left. Wiping his mouth with the back of his hand, he stood up and brushed himself off. The dirt and leaves had helped somewhat, but he had still been cold. It probably wasn't that smart of an idea to leave his pack back there, but he had been in such a hurry to get going. And he was also pretty much in shock at the time. At least he had grabbed the energy bars. He took one out of his pocket. *Good thinking.*

Looking around him, it was hard to believe anything had happened. The trees stood solid and strong in the early light. Green leafy plants stood their ground on the fir needles, and the sun was rising above the surrounding peaks.

Scott made his way out of the bushes and headed west. The cool mountain air braced him. He remembered the trail was in that direction and, although there was green foliage everywhere and trees and rocks, he knew the sunrise didn't lie. He picked his way over the uneven terrain. He was careful to not make too much noise and when he came to a clearing, he looked around before he traveled through. *Be aware of your surroundings*, he could almost hear his dad's voice. He had more than just himself to get out; he had to get his dad and Sally help, too.

Unlike Spanish Camp where they had hiked into the wilderness, this part of the Pasayten had fewer trees and was a wide-open area with lots of rocks and grassy flower-filled meadows. If the circumstances weren't so bad, it would be almost fairy-tale like, but it was hard to think fairy tale when things were life and death. Scott kept on walking.

Chapter Twenty-Five

Cassie and Terri drove the forest road to Billy Goat Trailhead. "We're almost there," said Cassie. "I wonder if the outfitter's going to be up there."

"Wow," said Terri, "A real Pasayten outfitter! How cool!"

"Yes, they have a corral, and they pack the dudes and supplies up and take them to their camp. They come and go at different times, so it's hard to say when they're up there."

Cassie pulled her truck to the end of the road. The corrals sat empty on one side and a camping area was on the other side of the road. A few trucks with campers and empty horse trailers behind sat in the parking lot.

"Well, I guess we're not the only ones up here." said Terri, looking at the other vehicles.

"It's a short season in the summer, so recreational horsemen and hikers are usually coming about now. Unless, of course, they are going to hit hunting season later on. That increases your chances of encountering early snow, so it's better now." Cassie expertly parked her truck and trailer. "Come on, Sammy," she called as she opened the back door. Her Border Collie bounded out, happy to finally get out after the long drive.

The women unloaded their horses and set them up on the highline.

"We can get all of our stuff ready this afternoon, and tomorrow early we'll get packed up and on our way. I don't like to try to do a pack in the same day I get to the trailhead. Nothing ever seems to go right when you do it that way."

"Hey, I'm just happy to get this far." Terri laughed. "What can I do to help set up?"

"Well, get your gear out and we can start organizing. We'll just sleep in the bed of the truck tonight so we don't have to bother with unpacking our tents, or anything. You did bring an extra sleeping bag like I told you, right?"

"You bet. I've got it right here." Terri pulled it out of her gear bag.

The women worked very well together, and Cassie was once again glad she had met Terri. They had already made a list at home of what they were going to bring, so now it was just a matter of taking their scale and weighing the boxes and bags to make sure they had everything of equal weight on each side of the packs.

"You got your boxes packed with all the heavy stuff down at the bottom, too, right?

"Oh, yeah. And I also made sure to have less weight in my top pack than my two side packs." Terri picked up each of her pack boxes checking the weight and then set them back down again. "Yup, feels about equal."

Cassie laughed. "I do believe I'm seeing a packer here."

"Well, I certainly hope so; otherwise I've come a long ways for nothing."

The women stowed their gear back in the horse trailer until morning, built a small fire, and then set up their collapsible lawn chairs by the fire. Just as they were enjoying a cup of coffee they heard voices. They looked up and saw a group of kids with two adults and a black and white llama coming down the trail.

"Hello," called out Cassie.

"Dad, more horses. Look out for Lilah," cautioned one of the boys.

"Don't worry about our horses; they're all tied up for the night. They won't bother your

llama," assured Cassie.

"What happened? Did you have a bad experience on the trail with a horse?" asked Terri curiously.

The tallest boy of the kids said, "It was a black devil."

"Oh, my," said Cassie.

"Richard, now that is not a nice thing to say about horses to these ladies," his dad reprimanded him. "Not all horses are like that one."

"A black devil, huh? The guy riding it wouldn't be brown haired and mustached, and he wouldn't be riding with an olive-skinned guy, would he?" asked Cassie.

"How would you know that?" asked the man. He wrinkled his forehead and looked directly at Cassie.

"And the brown-haired guy is riding the black devil and pulling a white packhorse?"

"Exactly," said the man. He stood back a little bit in surprise.

"It's a small community of packers, so we do know each other a good bit of the time and our stock."

Terri looked at her, eyebrows raised.

"It would seem that Dusty and Mike are headed in the same trail we are," said Cassie.

"What a small world!" exclaimed Terri.

The little group turned to leave.

"Yes it is," Cassie agreed quietly.

Cassie sat staring into the fire. *I can't even go into the Pasayten and get away from him. That is so annoying! Well, I don't care if Dusty decided to come here, too. This is Terri and my trip and that is one thing he won't be taking from me.*

She turned her attention back to Terri and tried to push Dusty out of her thoughts. "So are you going to be up for a 22-mile ride tomorrow? I thought we could hit the meadow at Peevy Pass. There's a really nice camp in there."

"You bet. Just lead the way."

"There's camp water in a creek. If you want to go fishing later on, we can always hit Quartz Lake. I've heard rumors that there are some really, really huge fish in the bottom of that lake."

"Pasayten fish. I can't wait."

"Well, o-dark thirty comes early. I'm going to bed."

They banked their fire and climbed into their sleeping bags in the back of the pickup truck.

Chapter Twenty-Six

When Dusty woke he could see the sun shining on the canvas of his tent. The horses were already out. He could hear the rip, rip, munch and the small tinkle of the bell around Cheyenne's neck.

"Hey, is there coffee on?" he called out.

"Of course. What do you take me for?" yelled Mike. "It's morning, isn't it?"

"Well, had to make sure it was worth getting up. Be right there."

Scout was already out by the fire. The lake nearby was still with early morning mist rising like steam from the surface. The mountains stood tall all around them, their peaks devoid of snow, but prominent granite rock shone in the early morning sun.

Dusty threw on his Schafer coat and slipped on his Romeos, leaving his packer boots in his tent for the time being. His boots were great on the trail, but if his horses got in trouble in the middle of the night, he always brought his Romeos so he could just slip them on in a hurry. It was nice, too, not to have to lace up anything the minute you woke up in the morning. He put his hat on, stepped out of the tent and closed it up behind him.

As he walked to the fire, that comfortable feeling of being home washed over him. He grabbed the coffee pot off the rock warming by the fire and filled his cup. He turned and watched his horses as they grazed on the hillside. Corral Lake was in what packers would call a "hole." It wasn't a real hole, but it was recessed down a steep switchbacked trail on one side, and then sloped down into pine and fir forest below. The irregularity of the Pasayten was in full display here, with the arid, treeless area above them descending to the lake ringed with meadow grass and trees. Corral Lake itself, like many of the lakes in the wilderness, was grassy on one end, deep in the middle, with a shallow bottom around most of the shore.

Fishing was usually pretty good. Some years better than others. Dusty sat quietly finishing his coffee. Then making his mind up, he stood and put his cup down.

"I think I'm going to go check out the fish population this morning."

Dusty grabbed his pole and bait and walked over to the lake. He expertly planted a cast and the spinner hit the water with a resounding plop. He slowly began reeling it in. It didn't take long. The fish were hungry after the long winter and struck at his lure. After a couple of tentative strikes, the tip of his pole bent and stayed that way, bobbing up and down. He reeled it in, careful to play the fish and keep him on the line. The rainbow trout he pulled in was every bit of 18 inches long.

"Well, Scout, it looks like this is a one-fish morning."

Scout lay in the grass next to him watching the whole process.

Dusty set his pole down and set about cleaning his catch, careful to throw the guts far away from the water's edge. He put the fish through his stringer and headed back to camp.

Mike was still by the fire as Dusty and Scout came back.

"Well, the great hunter returns," said Mike. "That was quick."

"Yeah, almost too quick. Kind of like picking it up at the store." Dusty laid his fish down on the roll-a-table.

"That's a big one!"

"Yup, second cast. Man, I love this place."

113

After breakfast Dusty headed down to pick up his horses. The grass was so lush they hadn't traveled far, and full, they stood contentedly dozing in the early morning sunshine. He quickly slipped the hobbles off Cheyenne and Muley and clipped on their lead lines. As he walked back into camp, Mike was already saddling his horse.

"Are you going to leave one here?" asked Dusty.

"Yeah, as long as you are. We'll be able to cover a lot more ground without pulling a packhorse."

"It ought to be fine. Ginnie's got both of hers down below."

The common practice for packing in was to leave the packhorses on the highline during the day, with hobbles on their front feet so they didn't paw and tear up the forest floor. They could stand, lie down and move around so they wouldn't get stiff. Horses, being grazing animals, had the ability to sleep on their feet. They could rock back on their tendons and get a nap without even lying down, so it was a lot more comfortable for them than it looked.

The re-introduction of wolf packs and the increased population of cougars due to the no-dogs hunting regulations made leaving the horses more of a concern. But having Ginnie and her stock close by, and the presence of people in the immediate vicinity, Dusty felt it was safe to leave the stock. At least so far the predators hadn't gotten that bold. Nothing to say that wouldn't change in the future as the wolf packs got bigger and the animals more aggressive, or as the cougars multiplied and food became scarce.

Dusty tied Cheyenne up to the highline and turned back to Muley. He thought to himself as he brushed his horse, *There is something to be said about making the wolves protected and the cougars almost impossible to find without the aid of hunting dogs...none of it good, either.*

"Boy, you'd think those guys would be a lot smarter and not signal every cougar and wolf in the area, neighing their brains out that we are leaving them," said Mike, turning his horse around as he waited for Dusty to mount.

"Yeah, I know. As smart as they are in some areas, they really fall short in others."

"I still like the part that they think they have to let us ride them." Mike chuckled. "I wouldn't want them to get any smarter about that."

"That's for sure." Dusty swung into the saddle. "Well, what do you say we stop by Uncle Bob's and see what they have got going on?"

"Let's do it." They turned their horses on the trail out of Corral Lake, the loud whinnying from the two horses left behind bouncing off the mountain walls.

The trail switchbacked out of Corral Lake, followed the ridge a short distance and then dropped down into Crow. The drop wasn't as far as it was into Corral, and they were there in about 15 minutes.

The outfit's white canvas tents came into sight. The biggest one had a black chimney with smoke pouring out of it, the mess tent. The dudes' horses were already in stages of being saddled, and people were picking up their lunch sacks from the table and finishing up their coffee.

Everyone stopped and stared as Dusty and Mike rode into camp. A man in his 60s with white hair and a brown cowboy hat stopped currying a horse.

"Well, I'll be darned. Look what the cat drug in," the man quickly walked over to Muley.

Dusty swung out of the saddle in one smooth movement, and he and his uncle were in

a powerful bear hug. The men slapped each other on the back and took a step back.

"I wondered when I'd be seeing you up here." The older man's suntanned face crinkled in a big smile.

"You knew I couldn't stay away, Uncle Bob. It sure is good to see you."

"We were just getting saddled up for a day trip over to Quartz Lake. Maybe you two would like to come back around tonight for dinner?" said Uncle Bob. "Andy has got something special cooking, and Ginnie's going to be over."

"Yes, so we heard," said Dusty.

"It's a small wilderness, isn't it?" Mike joined the conversation.

"And there's your sidekick," said Bob, "How are you doing, Mike?" Bob and Mike warmly shook hands.

Mike gave a big grin. "Since I got up here I've been doing really fine."

"Yeah, the backcountry has a way of doing that to a person, that's for sure."

The dudes had gathered around to watch—a family, a middle-aged husband and wife, a woman in her 20s and an older gentlemen with a camera and fisherman hat on.

Andy, the cook, came out of the mess tent, wiping his hands on a dishcloth. "Hi, Dusty. Long time no see."

"It's always good to see you, Andy. And the emphasis is on the always." Dusty laughed.

"Oh, and would that be around mealtime particularly?" joked Andy.

"Well, particularly that time, yes. Well, we don't want to hold you guys up, so we'll come back tonight." Dusty gathered up his reins and swung easily back into the saddle. "Come on, Scout."

"Have a good ride." Mike turned his horse and followed Dusty on the trail leading out of Crow Lake.

"What a cute, well-mannered dog," they heard the older woman exclaim as they rode away.

Chapter Twenty-Seven

Despite the cold night, Sally slept hard, and when she opened her eyes in the dim light, it took her a few minutes to remember where she was. She sat up and listened. She had no watch, but the sun was peeking over her rock fortress.

Sally crawled out from under her hiding place. She was greeted with sunshine, blue clear sky and white snowy peaks around her. The sun felt good. It appeared to be midmorning. She was glad to have her light sweatshirt over her tank top; luckily she hadn't taken it off on their morning hike yesterday. She shivered. The thought of the hike brought back the nightmare of the prior morning. It still was difficult to assimilate. *How could I have gone from suburban Seattleite to this person alone in the wilderness?* Well, it was what it was, and it wouldn't help to think about it. She had to get out.

With a new resolve, Sally stood up and brushed off the leaves and dirt. She looked around at the forested mountains and valleys stretching as far as the eye could see, picked a path that she hoped was in the opposite direction of the men, and started walking. The birds were chirping and the mountain flowers bloomed all around her. It was actually pretty relaxing, and the presence of bad men and bears seemed far away.

Sally hadn't been hiking long when she came to a creek. She sat by the side and scooped a drink from a swiftly flowing riffle. The mountain water was clear and cold, and it helped with the hunger that was once again grinding in her stomach.

She stood up and stretched, she felt better and started to walk.

A voice shouted out, "Thar she is, Clem, right over thar!" And a crashing through the brush followed. Sally's insides froze.

"Don't let her get away this'n time, Tom!" a second voice followed.

Sally sprinted through the forest with fear fueling her as she was ducking under logs and jumping over fallen trees.

Tom and Clem had crazy on their side, they were determined not to lose their prey this time. They had spent a lot of time hunting in the woods, and this was no different to them.

"Damn, I wish we had the dogs," huffed Tom.

"Circle wide and we'll cut her off. She doesn't know what direction she's headin'," wheezed out Clem.

"Will do." Tom cut off to the right, where the countryside sloped down and he could take cover in the trees and cut back in at a different angle.

Sally only could think in survival mode: *Run, Run, Run.* Instead of going through the meadows, she struck for the cover of the trees. Who knew if they would try to shoot her? They definitely were armed for it.

The chase went on for what seemed like hours. Her heart beat against her chest like a bass drum. Her breathing was ragged. She leaped over a couple of flat rocks. Below her yawned a 50-foot drop, a waterfall and a roaring river. Sally instinctively grabbed hold of the trees on either side to stop herself from plunging over the edge.

"We got 'er now, Tom!" a shout erupted not far behind her.

A second's hesitation. She might die if she jumped. She would die for sure if she didn't.Sally pushed herself off the ledge. She aimed as far off the rocks as she could, toward the middle of the deep pool at the bottom of the falls. The drop seemed to take forever. The wind roared in her ears. Then she hit with a big splash. The icy water closed over her head. Down, down she went. She felt herself descending the bottomless pool. A panic was building in her chest.

Finally, after what seemed an eternity, her feet hit the rocky sand. Sally pushed off with her lungs bursting and hit the surface gasping for air. The frigid water felt like a vise on her head. For a second the pool held her still. Then she felt herself being pulled under. She fought against it. The current snatched her and threw her downstream. Her body was thrown around like a ragdoll. She bounced off the bottom and then was catapulted to the surface again. The river possessed her with such a fury she became disoriented. She grasped at branches.

"Never stand up in the river." The guide's voice from a long ago raft trip echoed. Her body bounced off a rock. Pain burned up her hip. "The current can be deceiving."

A turbulent force pulled her head-over-heels under the water. Her hands scrabbled at the rocks on the bottom. *Push! Up!* With a Superwoman heave, Sally pushed off the bottom. White lights exploded in her head. Her lungs would burst! Then, air. Blessed air. She flailed her arms and legs to stay in the middle of the river. All the blowdown lay on the shores and it was certain death if she was swept underneath anything. The river pounded in her head like a freight train. *I have to get out!*

Sally dug deep with a makeshift crawl stroke to guide her. She rolled and slammed off a couple of smaller rocks. Excruciating pain shot through her shoulder. The channel narrowed between two gigantic boulders, and the river picked up speed. Sally flew between the boulders, momentarily airborne. Then she dropped about three feet into a huge pool. The main flow cascaded off to the left, she found herself in a calm eddy with a sandy shore. She paddled over to the edge and clawed her way out. As she lay there, every bone in her body ached. The cold receded into numbness.

Thank you, God, was all she could think. She was still alive! She had heard of so many drownings. It was unfathomable the undertow hadn't taken her. Or bashed her head against the rocks.

The sun warmed her back and she lay for a few minutes trying to recuperate. As the reality of her situation came back to her, she knew she had to move. Thinking of those disgusting animals finding her was so repulsive her adrenaline kicked in. She kneeled, then rose to a standing position. A wave of dizziness washed over her. Her knees buckled. Panting, she hung onto a nearby boulder. As she looked around, she saw she was standing on a little sandy beach around the rocks. The forest came down to the shores of the river. The trees were thick and dark. The edges fanned out at a mild slope and blended into more forest for as far as the eye could see.

Sally heard the birds chirping and the crickets buzzing. A good sign she was alone. She found her bearings at a point on the far edge of the forest and took a deep breath. *Crazy, the dip in the river actually was kind of refreshing.* It must be true: *What doesn't kill you only makes you stronger. Either that or I'm finally losing my mind!* "Whatever," she said aloud, and hiked into the forest.

Clem stood above the falls where Sally had jumped. He was completely baffled. *How in the hell did she do that?* All that lay 50 feet below him was the waterfall and the pool with water swirling and foam on the shores. He saw her with his own eyes! She was right there and she jumped! But where did she go? There were rocks around the pool and she would have had to hit it just right to not land on any of those. What would be the chances of that? Whatever the chances were, Clem knew that they were more than he would be willing to take. Still, where was her body? He squinted, and he could still see nothing. He heard the roar of the waterfall and felt light spray on his face. The smell of fresh melted snow rose in his nostrils.

As he stood staring out, Tom came stumbling up behind him. "What happened to her?"

"That's what I'm tryin' ta figure out," Clem said. "One minute she was here and the next minute, gone."

"Should we follow along the bank fer a bit just to make sure?"

"Yeah, we'd better. People just don't dis'pear."

The two men crawled along the steep hillside over logs and ferns until they made it down to the river. The banks were untouched and a deep green pool bubbled and swirled. They walked down the shores of the creek for a mile or so until they came to the large boulders. The flow narrowed and deepened through the passage and then it shot out into a pool, smaller than the one under the falls. Fallen logs lay on the sides of the creek, with branches and other forest accumulations.

Clem and Tom crawled higher on the bank to get around the boulders, and then they saw the sand that surrounded the pool. As they made their way over rocks and logs to investigate, they grabbed onto small trees and whatever else they could find to not fall headfirst down the hill. At the bottom they studied the sand.

"Well, I'll be damned! Take a look at this, Clem!" Tom gestured at the sand.

"I got eyes, Tom," snapped Clem. "Looks like our little girl can fly and swim if'n she needs to."

Tom clapped his hands together. "This is getting to be more fun than a coon hunt!"

"Yeah, well, why don't you save the clappin' for when we actually git 'er."

Knee and hand imprints in the sand showed where Sally had pulled herself out of the creek. A couple of small footprints disappeared into the rocks and brush. Clem and Tom didn't waste any time and headed into the woods following the direction of the prints.

Chapter Twenty-Eight

Dusty and Mike rode out of Crow Lake onto the trail.

"Where to, Boss?"

"What do you say we head over to Sheep Lake and check out the fishing."

"That sounds good. Are we going down or up Dead Horse Pass?"

"How about up it? I want to check out the old trapper cabin on the way in and see who's been through," said Dusty.

The old trapper cabin at Sheep Lake had been there forever. It still held the shape of a short-walled cabin, but it had a secret that only the old packers knew about. When you opened up the door and looked at the back, there was a registry of a who's who in the packer world. Everyone for years had signed and dated it. Dusty's name had been there since he was 12 years old and his Uncle Bob had shown it to him. Boy, he had really felt like he belonged after that!

The two men rode along the trail, remaining in the open country and skirting the side of the mountains. Small creeks trickled and babbled as they rode past foot bridges. Indian paintbrush and lupine were just pushing up, and the scents were fresh and plentiful. The views, as Dusty looked around them, were all mountains. Peaks in front of peaks that extended off into the Canadian border.

"Whenever I look up at those mountains I always think of Louis L'Amour and the Blue Mountains he'd always talk about in his books."

"Yep. That would fit here for sure." Mike rode with a loose rein and sat relaxed in the saddle. Both men had spent many, many hours riding; for them it was even more comfortable than walking.

Muley acted like he hadn't even walked a block, let alone the 18-plus miles he'd just completed to get into Corral Lake. There was a lot of benefit to having a horse in shape. People viewed horses in different ways, depending on how they wanted to use them. Dusty and Mike wanted tough horses that could handle quick changes in weather and difficult terrain. They kept their horses out in the pasture with only a lean-to for shelter in extreme heat or snow. They never blanketed the horses unless they were trailering after a hot ride in the cold, or if they were in real cold weather. Their horses were used to it and very hardy. Dusty could not remember the last time he or Mike had a sick or lame horse. It just didn't happen.

Of course, once in a while in the high county a horse would pull a shoe stepping into a hole or catching it just right on a snag. That was where Mike came in; he was pretty handy at nailing on horseshoes. He always carried a few extra nails and a fencing tool. Not only was the tool handy for cutting fence wire, but it was also good for nailing on shoes—a two in one.

As they rode along the trail cut through grassy meadows. Several times Muley thought it would be a good place to eat, but Dusty let him know that wasn't in the game plan just yet.

"Okay. It's right in here somewhere. Keep a sharp eye for the trail," he cautioned.

Mike scanned the meadow."Will do, Boss."

It didn't take long before they saw the narrow furrow in the grass of an old trail. These were not standard Forest Service trails, so they were not maintained. They were classified user trails, which was a misnomer since the Forest Service didn't want them used at all. The more time Dusty spent in the mountains, the more familiar he became with the location of these trails.

The men rode down a slope through the grass and scrub trees. Over a little rise, a cabin stood in a small clearing. Dusty and Mike dismounted and tied their horses. They walked over to the cabin and opened the door.

"Been pretty busy up here since the last time we were here," said Mike.

After scanning names and dates from way down at the bottom all the way to the top, they remounted and rode the short distance to the lake.

Dusty surveyed the shore. "Does this look like a good place to have lunch?"

"Good as any."

They slipped the bridles off their horses and tied them to a tree. Getting their lunches out of their saddle bags, they walked over to the lake.

The lake was a typical alpine lake, shallow and surrounded by several large gray rocks. What was different was at the far end of the lake lay a huge rock formation that climbed several thousand feet to the top of the hill. It appeared as if the lake had been hewn out of rock.

Mike and Dusty sat on a boulder in the summer afternoon sun and threw an occasional bread crumb into the lake. It was snapped up immediately. They could see the shimmer of scales as the hungry fish slid through the water.

"Figures I didn't bring my fishing pole, doesn't it?

"Yeah, Murphy's law," agreed Mike.

After lunch they rode past the lake.

"So, are you ready for Dead Horse Pass?"

"Bring her on," said Mike.

Dead Horse Pass was another user trail not maintained by the Forest Service. It got its name from the obvious—a horse had died going down it. The trail was narrow, but readily distinguishable through the brush. As they rode the trail quickly gained altitude, narrowing perceptively as it climbed. The only encouragement was a single horse's hoofprints in the trail in front of them, so someone at least had gone before them. Even though Dusty knew the trail was really a trail that led to a destination, it could be impassable—a tree could have fallen, rocks, debris, who knew what? And once a rider got to a certain point, there really was nowhere to turn around, since the trail narrowed to about twelve inches in some places, with a steep drop-off on the outside. Nevertheless, they continued on. The lake became a small greenish-blue dot below them. The altitude made Dusty's senses tingle and keeping balance while Muley climbed the narrow rugged trail gave him an adrenaline rush.

"Who says trail riding is boring, anyway?"

"The people who haven't ridden with us," Mike laughed.

As they entered a thicket of trees, Dusty saw the sign on the left, "Devil's Stairway."

"Hey," Mike said, "How come everything cool has to be devil stuff, anyway?"

"I don't know, but it seems like it, doesn't it?" said Dusty, thinking about the Seven Devils in Idaho and Satan's Wash Basin up at White Pass.

"Never Heaven's Gates, or anything like that," grumbled Mike.

The trail quickly left the trees behind and rose higher and higher. Just a few switchbacks beneath the top of the hill they saw a huge snowdrift.

"Uh-oh," said Mike.

The trail had become way too narrow to do anything but go forward.

"We are going through," said Dusty. "After all, we did see those hoofprints."

Mike, knowing Muley, had absolutely no doubt they would. He had seen that unbelievable horse jump up four-foot-high flat walls of snow. Muley had a bond with Dusty and all Dusty had to do was point him and he did it. Mike could not remember ever seeing such a strong connection between a man and his horse.

As they closed the gap to the top of the mountain, they found a trail that just skirted the snowdrift and up and over the sidehill they went. As they stood on the top and looked around, the views filled Dusty's soul. Mike and he were quiet and stared over the wide expanse they had scaled.

"Well, look here." Dusty rode up next to a horse skull on a rock. "Guess this is the namesake for the trail."

Mike rode up next to him and looked down at the skull. "So glad we didn't have to join him. On this trip, anyway."

"Or many more to come," agreed Dusty. "Well, I suppose we ought to head back and see what Uncle Bob's got cooking for dinner."

"Lead the way, Boss. I'm right behind you."

They headed down the grassy slope toward the main trail that would lead them back to camp. The sun was just above the mountain peaks on the horizon. The crickets chirped in the late afternoon warmth.

Chapter Twenty-Nine

Scott had been walking for a long time. The sun slipped across the sky, toasting his back. He wasn't sure how far he'd come, but he knew by his dad's pedometer that he averaged about two miles an hour. Scott could go faster than that, but he didn't want to get too tired and dehydrated. Drinking water with no purifier was risky, so he drank just enough from the many creeks along the way to keep going.

Scott began to falter, but he slowly put one foot in front of the other. He could block out the ever-present hunger, but lack of sleep was getting to him. The countryside, as beautiful as it was, began to take on a similarity. He did his best to keep himself headed in one direction. Scott knew it was easy enough to go in circles, so he tried to guard against it. Rocks, dirt, trees and meadows, over and over. Then he saw it. A trail. It appeared to be well worn and not a game path. Scott felt hope course through his veins. He suppressed the urge to cry out. Finally. He hiked on, looking for trail signs. This was not the way he had come in, so it was all new country to him. One thing he was sure of; eventually trails were going to lead to people and help.

Scott had not taken a bath since his dip in the lake a couple days ago. He was filthy with dirt from the trail and from covering himself with anything he could find for warmth at night. His arm throbbed. The makeshift sling he made kept it from banging, but the skin was hot and swollen. Scott felt feverish, but he couldn't let that get in his way, he told himself. His dad and sister depended on it. The trail stretched out ahead of him, taking its time meandering through grassy valleys and winding through rocks and small berry bushes. It was colorful with a splashing of wildflowers everywhere. In spite of his pain and disorientation, Scott stopped for a moment in amazement. *How could something so bad happen in such a beautiful place?* It was so sudden too. One minute their family had been hiking down the trail planning what they would do when they got home, and the next minute everything changed. Of all the possible dangers Scott had considered when he had planned this trip with his dad and sister, people danger was not one he had thought of. Scott knew that he would never look at strangers the same way again after this.

Thankfully, the weather was still warm. Scott figured it to be late afternoon. He hoped he found out where he was, or ran into somebody before it turned dark again. If he didn't, he would have to spend yet another night without a sleeping bag or anything else to protect him from the elements. He certainly could not keep going down the trail in the dark; for sure he would probably get lost or fall and injure himself further.

Scott tried to remember the map and the possible area he might be in. He didn't see how he could be that far off track. Wherever this trail led, he would find out pretty soon. And that gave him hope.

Chapter Thirty

Cassie checked her packs. She made sure the lash cinch was tight. Oftentimes after loading her packhorse, she'd find enough room to put her fist through it. She thought about when she was being taught how to pack to enter the BCHW Packer's Rendezvous so many years ago.

"Cut them in half," the old packer would tell her. "A little gal like you ain't never gonna get it too tight, anyway."

She chuckled to herself. He probably had never seen her throw bales of hay. And while she didn't mind making sure the cinch was tight, the thought of actually cutting her horse in half was not a pretty picture.

"Terri, you ready?"

"Oh, yeah. Do I look ready?" Terri had her two horses' lead ropes in hand. Her packhorse was packed and mantied. Her riding horse was saddled, bridled, and her slicker and warm coat tied on.

"I'd say it's official," said Cassie, "I'm looking at a real Pasayten packer!"

Terri's perpetual grin widened even more. "Well, then, let's head 'em up and move 'em out."

"Let's," agreed Cassie, as she lightly swung into the saddle. Riding up to the trailhead, Cassie double checked that her keys were safely in her pommel bag. She always brought all her important possessions; checkbook, credit cards, and wallet, and put them in her saddlebags. Not that she'd need any of them up here, but it was foolhardy to leave them in the truck. Trailhead vandalism had sadly reached a new high, and Cassie wasn't going to reward them when they broke into her rig.

As they arrived at the trailhead kiosk, Cassie dismounted and filled out a trail permit indicating how many in their party, including dogs. Sammy bounded up next to her as she bent over the wooden desk filling out the form.

"Don't worry, Sammy, I wouldn't forget about you." She stopped to scratch her dog's head.

Filling out the trailhead permits was important. It let the Forest Service know who was out on the trails and what the destinations and dates of arrival and departure would be. If somebody came up missing, that information came in handy. For horsemen there was an even better reason—to be counted. One of the popular arguments to eradicate horses from the wilderness was the horsemen weren't using the backcountry, anyway, or in too few numbers to make a difference. That was not true, but the flip side of that was that horsemen were not big on paperwork. It was a whole lot easier just to ride by the kiosk than to fill out the permit. Oftentimes the kiosks were empty, all the permits were gone, or there was no pen or pencil to fill them out. Cassie circumvented this problem by carrying her own supply of permits and a pen.

She pulled off the carbon copy and put it into the slot provided and then tied the permit on her horse. She remounted and turned her horse down the trail.

"How long do you figure until we hit Peevy Pass?" asked Terri.

"It's about 22 miles, so not before 3 or 3:30, as long as we keep up the pace."

"That's no problem."

Their horses were in excellent shape and they were averaging about three miles per hour on their last count. They hadn't gone very far when they came to a large creek crossing where they let their horses drink. The trail was wooded and views were limited except for an occasional glimpse of a snowcapped peak.

"The trees don't disappear until about 12 miles down the trail, then everything opens up," said Cassie, pulling her horse's head up. "That's enough for now, Prince. We don't want you to colic."

"I can't wait," bubbled Terri, "But this is pretty cool, too."

As they rode through the woods and deeper into the wilderness, Cassie began to relax. The smell of the horses and the crisp fir trees was a drug that couldn't be bottled, sold and made a profit from—it was free. She felt so fortunate to have this escape. Cassie really enjoyed the law, but the frustrations of an imperfect system gnawed away at her. Her dad had pointed out to her years ago that just because she thought something was fair didn't mean everyone would agree with her. It was a hard concept for her to grasp, especially after passing the bar. The law was supposed to be black and white. Cassie looked behind her to make sure her load and pack animal were secure. But why did it have so many possible outcomes that it had a lot more to do with the skill of the lawyer than the actual case presented?

Out here in the wilderness, none of those things mattered. The mountains stood majestically with their snow-shrouded tops, and the trees stood silent with only an occasional wind riffling through their branches. There was no judgment. Everything was exactly as it appeared. Cassie could feel the stress leave her body, her neck and shoulders relaxing. She hadn't even realized that she had been so stiff. She could ride for hours and never get sore, but give her a trial, and she could really feel it after a day or two.

Involuntarily, her mind went back to the case with Dusty Rose. It annoyed her, because that was one of the things she came up here to forget about—and then here he was. The wilderness wasn't even big enough to get rid of him. He was an attractive man; that was a given. But he had such an easy way about him, it was so frustrating. He walked into court late and, without being in a rush, calmly pulled his paperwork out of his briefcase, smiling at the clerk and court reporter. While her palms were sweating and she kept going over her argument in her mind, he was laughing and talking to his client.

The argument she gave she felt was flawless. At one point she truly forgot to breathe, but she'd recovered, and it actually came out as a heartfelt presentation of the law for her client and his small family business. She knew it had. When it was Dusty's turn, he had slowly ambled up to the bench, one hand in his pocket like he was going to address a good friend. He was engaging, articulate, and he shot her argument into little pieces with his "back home in Eagleclaw we do things this way" speech. The killer was, he was representing big business, not the little guy. At the end of his argument when she got up with rebuttal, she did her best, but the court ruled in Dusty's favor. How did he do that? She thought again about the last-minute photos and heat shot up her neck. She felt her shoulders begin to tighten up again and took a deep breath of mountain air. She was not going to let that ruin her trip. Work was work, a means to an end. And this was the end. She was going to enjoy herself now.

The women broke through the trees and entered an arid country with fresh mountain grass topping the hills and huge mountains all around them.

"Whoa. Is that Canada up that way?" Terri gestured at the mountains lining up behind each other as far as the eye could see until they turned dark blue and melted into the skyline.

"Yes, that turns into British Columbia at some point up there."

"I can't wait to see the border." Terri stood taller in her stirrups as if to catch a glimpse of it.

Cassie nodded. "It is really cool to look over into Canada right there at Border Lake. The only drawback is that they have roads that actually come right up to our border on their side, while on our side it's nonmotorized vehicles only and wilderness."

"That could be a problem with people sneaking over, couldn't it?" asked Terri.

"Well, they have Border Patrol and drones up there now. But yeah, if somebody wanted in, it probably wouldn't stop them. Just like our southern borders."

"Scary thought."

Cassie felt around her back for her .38 and gave it a pat. She also carried a Winchester .30-.30 rifle in a scabbard on her saddle. You just never knew, and it was better to be safe than sorry, she thought.

Both women grew silent, immersed in the beauty of the country around them. The only noise besides the horses' hooves was the occasional screech of a hawk overhead. The trail climbed up a slope with few switchbacks, but continued to gain a steady altitude. Reaching the top of the slope, the trail sign indicated a turnoff to Corral Lake. They continued on and soon looked down on the white tents of an outfitter's camp in the small heavily-treed basin that contained Crow Lake.

"I think that's Dusty Rose's uncle's outfit," said Cassie.

"Oh, really?" Terri looked down. Smoke drifted from the campfire, and the camp itself looked vacant.

"Yeah, they probably took the dudes out for a day ride, fishing or sightseeing somewhere."

They rode along the hillside for another couple of hours, crossing small bridges and riding up and down rises until they came to a fork in the trail. The trail sign indicated Quartz Lake, and they turned. After heading into the trees and switchbacking down for about 20 minutes, they came to an open meadow with lots of mountain grass and a strong creek running through it. A camp in the trees on the edge of the meadow stood vacant. It had a fire pit and was not very far from the stream.

"Here we are," said Cassie.

"This is beautiful." Terri turned in her saddle taking in the whole view.

They tied their horses up and dropped the packs off the packhorses first, then unsaddled. Tired as she was, Cassie always loved getting the camp set up and then sitting by the fire with a cup of coffee. It just didn't get any better than that.

Chapter Thirty-One

Scott had been walking for what seemed like forever. The dull pain thumped in his arm, and his feet were so blistered it was a toss-up as to which hurt worst. Leaving his boots on day and night with filthy socks had taken a toll. His feet heavy, he was now dragging them to put one foot in front of the other. His muscles were screaming to just lie down and rest for a while, but he knew if he did he might never get up again. It was that fear that kept him going. Finally he tripped on a rock and pitched headlong on the trail. He really wanted to get up again, but he was all in. He shut his eyes. Maybe he'd just rest a little bit.

Dusty and Mike rode down the user trail and turned onto the main trail. They were still enjoying the aftereffects of an adrenaline-pumped ride.

"Why is it that the best trails are never on the map?" said Mike. "That was definitely not a beginner ride."

"I guess that's the beauty of getting to know the land. The more experience you get, the more you are able to broaden your riding area."

They rode on as the sun began to light the back of the mountains.

"We might as well go to Uncle Bob's, since it's on the way, and just tie our horses up there."

"That's fine with me," said Mike. "The sooner we have dinner, the better."

The trail opened up into a big valley in the hillside, with a little creek and a bridge over it. It looked like a rock had fallen in the trail, lying in the shadow of the mountain. Dusty didn't think anything of it as he approached, and Scout trotted up to it to investigate. All of a sudden, about three feet away from the rock, Muley planted his feet and stood still, snorting.

"What the heck is that?" said Mike from the back.

The "rock" groaned. Dusty jumped off his horse, threw the reins over the saddle horn and ran over to where Scout stood. A dirt-encrusted boy lay curled up in a ball, either sleeping or unconscious, Dusty couldn't tell which. He gently touched the boy's arm. "Hey, there son, are you okay?"

The boy's eyes flew open. He looked blank for a minute and then fearful. "Who are you?" he croaked through chapped lips.

"My name's Dusty and this is my friend Mike."

The boy sat up, favoring his left arm tied in a dingy T-shirt. "My dad, my sister," he said breathlessly. "We've got to help them." The boy tried to get up, but he fell back down again.

"Just hold on there, Partner," cautioned Dusty. "Let's get you some water and something to eat first. Looks like you're all wore out." He stood and walked over to his saddlebags. Muley stood obediently ground-tied. Dusty grabbed an extra bottle of water and a couple energy bars from his bag.

Scout sat right next to the boy offering his warmth and moral support. Still dazed, the boy unconsciously patted him. Dusty opened the water and handed it to the boy.

He took it and drank from it greedily.

"Careful there, Son. You're going to make yourself sicker than you already are if you drink it too fast."

"I'm so thirsty."

"Take little sips. Try some of this." Dusty handed him the

unwrapped energy bar. "Take little bites of that, too."

Mike walked over and squatted next to the boy. "So where did you hike in from?"

"We came in from Spanish Camp," the boy said, the water and bar reviving him a little, "over at Andrews Creek Trailhead."

"Whoa," said Dusty, "You've come a long way."

The boy managed a faint smile, then worry crossed his face. "We got to get going. They've got my sister and dad."

"Who's got them?" said Mike.

"Bad men. They were on the trail. They hit my dad and grabbed my sister." Tears now streamed unchecked down his cheeks.

He had Dusty and Mike's full attention.

"When did this happen?" asked Dusty.

"A couple days ago. I went cross-country. Slept under rocks. So they wouldn't find me."

Dusty could see the boy was clearly traumatized and suffering from exposure and his injury, so he probably wasn't going to get a whole lot more detail from him. The sun was starting to slip behind the mountaintops and dusk was beginning to settle on them. "Let's get you back to camp, get some food, and let Andy and Uncle Bob take a look at that arm."

Dusty mounted Muley, "Mike, can you hand him up to me?"

"You bet, Boss."

Mike bent over and picked up the young boy, careful not to jar his arm. He gingerly handed him up to Dusty, who set him on the saddle in front of him. Scott groaned a bit at the movement. "Mister, I don't know how to ride a horse."

"My name's Dusty and this here's Mike," Dusty repeated for the second time. "If we're going to be riding partners, we ought to know each other's names. What's yours?"

"I'm Scott Ross," he answered through parched lips.

"Well, Scott, you just take it easy, and old Muley here will take care of the rest," assured Dusty.

As soon as Scott was on his back, Muley became a different horse. He took careful steps to keep his new load safe and in the middle. Dusty knew that for Muley only two things held a soft spot in his heart: Dusty and kids.

Scott was not very heavy, and Dusty easily slipped a hand around him, taking care not to touch his bad arm. Taking the reins in his free hand, they made their way down the trail.

"We're going to take you back to Uncle Bob's camp. They'll have a first-aid kit and be able to help you there. Mike and I will set out first thing in the morning to find your dad and your sister, so don't worry about that. You just need to rest and get that arm taken care of."

Scott felt himself relax for the first time in what seemed like weeks. These men seemed honest and they would help him. The rhythm of the horse walking and the smoky smell from Dusty's clothing made him feel safe. He started to doze off. The pain from his arm was still raw and pounding. He could feel the heat rising from his skin.

"Do you have some more water?" he croaked.

"I think you better just hold off a little bit and let what you've had so far settle. When we get back we'll get you something for that fever."

"'Kay," replied Scott and his eyes closed.

Chapter Thirty-Two

The trio wasn't far from Uncle Bob's camp and they made it there in less than an hour. Riding over the top of the hill, Dusty saw a buzz of activity. The dudes were back from their day ride and all the horses had been turned out to graze. Smoke trailed from the stovepipe in the wall cook tent and more arose from the fire. People gathered around the campfire, laughing and talking. The temperature would be dropping soon. No matter how warm it was in the day, the Pasayten could get very cold at night. Dusty couldn't count how many times he had lain down to a warm evening in his tent, only to find snow on the ground the next morning.

As soon as Uncle Bob saw Dusty with the additional rider, he and a couple of his wranglers came running up.

"Dusty, what have you got there? Was there an accident?"

"Uncle Bob, this is Scott Ross. And yes, we need to have his arm looked at right away."

"Jim, you go get Andy and the first-aid kit. I'll help Dusty," ordered Bob.

Muley stood stock still while Dusty handed off Scott to Bob, who carefully took him and carried him over to a wall tent. Scout trotted along at his heels and then lay down outside of the tent.

Dusty turned to his riding partner. "Mike, would you mind taking Muley so I can talk to Bob?"

"No problem, Boss." Mike took the reins from Dusty. He walked the horses a short distance away, left the saddles on, but stripped off their bridles and put on their hobbles so they could graze.

The dudes had set their coffee and wine down and hurried over to watch the excitement.

"What happened to the boy? Why is he alone?"

"Don't know yet," said Bob, walking back from the tent. "This is big country and anything can happen. We'll let him rest up a little, get some food in him and then see if we can find out."

Everyone went back to the campfire and subdued conversation continued.

The camp cook, Andy, went into the tent with the first-aid kit. Bob followed him in.

"I've got some water boiling. We'll get that arm cleaned up and see what we have. It looks like it might be a break." He tore off Scott's sleeve and took a look. He got a thermometer out of the first-aid kit and put it in Scott's mouth. The boy was burning up with fever.

"Let me know what you think. I've got the SPOT Satellite if we need an airlift." Bob held the small mechanical device in his hand.

The thermometer buzzed after a little bit, and Andy pulled it out. "We're going to need to ice him." He walked over to Bob and said quietly, "Better activate the airlift."

"Will do." Bob hurried out the tent door to activate the Spot Satellite, a small handheld device that transmitted an SOS to the Forest Service and Medevac Flights.

"I've got an area marked out here for an airlift. Just in case," he smiled at the dudes. "Don't worry, this is the first time I've used it." Bob walked out into the open meadow and laid the satellite down on the ground. The SOS light was beeping steady green, which affirmed the signal had been transmitted successfully.

The wrangler, Jim, brought in hot water and Andy carefully began cleaning Scott's arm.

Dusty was still standing in the tent. "Scott, can you tell me anything about where you were camping at?"

Scott moaned, "My head is pounding. Oww!"

"I know it hurts," said Andy, "but we can't really give you anything for the pain right now. We've got to wait for the paramedics."

Dusty could see Scott frowning. He looked like he was trying hard to concentrate. "It was at a lake. I went fishing." His voice sounded faint.

It was a start, although there were so many lakes in the Pasayten, it really didn't help.

"Do you remember the name of the lake, Scott?" Dusty looked at him intently.

"It was..." Scott's young dirty face tensed with the effort. "It was greenish-blue in the middle and shallow. We had our tent. Went to the border at Canada and saw lots of flowers. My dad liked this band...the Ramones. Like that."

Dusty jumped right on it, "Ramon Lake?" There was a Remmel Lake too, but it was too far from the border.

"Yeah. We were hiking out of there. The bad men were waiting for us in the trail. They had horses. And guns."

Dusty's heart sank. *Drug runners.* Ramon Lake wasn't that far from the border. This was the first that he had ever heard of recreationalists being targeted for crime, but he guessed it was coming.

"Don't worry, Scott. I know just where that is, and we'll head out at first light," he assured the boy. "Meanwhile, you've come a long ways. You just take it easy. You're going to get a helicopter ride in just a little while."

"No," moaned Scott, "I need to find them."

"Listen, you're hurt. Andy here is going to get you cleaned up and we are going to get you to a hospital. Your dad and sister would want you to get help. You are just going to have to trust me on this one. Man to man, okay?" Dusty looked him in the eye.

"Let's shake on it."

Scott clenched his teeth and held out his good hand. Dusty carefully placed his hand in Scott's and they gently shook. "There. It's a sealed deal now, Scott. We will find your dad and sister."

"Thanks a lot, Dusty. I'll be back as soon as I can."

Dusty was impressed by the boy's tenacity. Despite his injuries and fatigue, his commitment to his family was first. It was a rare thing in today's world. His dad had done a good job raising him.

Dusty left the tent so Andy could get the boy comfortable and cleaned up as much as possible until the airlift got there. He went out to the fire. "Uncle Bob, you got any coffee?"

"Coffee pot is always on. Grab a cup and help yourself," his uncle replied.

"How's the boy doing?"

Dusty picked up a coffee cup off the table in the kitchen area and walked over to the fire where Uncle Bob sat with the older couple and a younger woman.

"He's still in pretty rough shape with that arm. Andy thinks it's a fracture. It looks like he's got some exposure from being out so long with no food and very little water, but he should be okay."

"Well, that's good news," said Bob. The dudes nodded.

"Only thing is, we're going to have to go out and look for the rest of his family. His dad and his sister got assaulted out there, it sounds like, and they all got separated. Mike and I are heading out first thing in the morning to find them."

Andy came out of the tent and walked to the fire area. "He's just about asleep now. He's had a rough couple of days and sleep is going to do him good."

"That's good," said Uncle Bob. "When the paramedics get here, we can see about getting his mother's name and phone number so they can have her waiting when he lands."

"Will do," said Andy. "And now I'd better get back to cooking."

Mike walked up to the fire. "Go right to it, Andy. We sure don't want to hold you up on that." He grinned.

"Absolutely," agreed Dusty. "We are going to need our strength for the search tomorrow."

"All right, all right." Andy threw up his arms in mock exasperation. "A man can only do so many things at once." Smiling, he walked back to the cook tent.

Chapter Thirty-Three

Mike helped himself to a cup of coffee and sat.

The dudes had been talking among themselves. The older woman asked, "Is that the nice forest ranger?" She pointed to the quickly approaching figure.

"Yes, it is," said Bob.

"Oh, wonderful. We really enjoyed meeting her," the woman exclaimed. The others all agreed and everyone settled into a friendly discussion around the campfire.

Just as Andy, with the help of the wranglers, brought the big Dutch ovens and sat them on the table, Ginnie walked into camp.

"I didn't miss anything, did I?" she asked.

"You got here just in time," said Bob.

"And that was no stroke of luck either." Ginnie laughed, "I could smell your good cooking all the way over at Corral Lake!"

Andy smiled. "Well, we always aim to please."

"We've had a situation arise here this afternoon," said Bob, "and the Forest Service is going to want to know about it. It's pretty serious."

Ginnie walked over and grabbed a plate. "Uh-oh, what happened?"

"Dusty and Mike went for a ride over to Sheep Lake, and they ended up finding a young boy on the trail with a broken arm and a pretty good case of exposure," said Bob.

"All alone?" Ginnie turned to face Dusty and Mike.

"Dinner's ready," Andy called. The dudes got up and lined single file by the Dutch ovens, serving themselves. Mike and Dusty stood at the end of the line behind the wranglers with Ginnie and Bob.

"They basically got bushwacked on the trail. A couple of men with horses were waiting for them when they rounded a corner. The young boy has been out in the woods by himself without his pack for a couple of days. He's not real sure of the time," Dusty said.

"Poor kid. Did you get his name? What kind of shape is he in?" Ginnie stopped ladling food on her plate and looked at Dusty.

"His name is Scott Ross. We did get that much information," said Dusty.

"We kind of thought it was better not to push him on anything else until we got him stabilized," added Mike.

"Yeah, he was pretty beat up. And it looks like he's got a broken arm, too," said Dusty.

"I activated my SPOT Satellite, so it shouldn't be too much longer before they land out there in the meadows," said Bob.

"Wow, you just can't turn your back for one minute around here. I'll radio in tomorrow and let the office know about the situation. We can talk to the airlift when they get here about activating a search and rescue team." Ginnie set her plate down on the table. "They can radio ahead to let the boy's mother know so she can meet him. Any idea how old he is?"

Dusty thought back on his own kids. "I'd say about 10 years old. He's a good kid."

"I'll take you to him if you'd like to talk to him. We need to bring him some grub while we're at it," Bob said. He had made his way up to the Dutch ovens and began ladling food onto a plate.

"Whoa, not too much," cautioned Ginnie. "You don't want him getting sick in the helicopter."

"Yeah, you're right." Bob scraped half of it back into the pot.

Dusty and Mike got their food and sat down on the end of one of the handmade log picnic tables covered with a plastic green and white checked tablecloth. Uncle Bob had made an area right outside of the cook tent with canvas awnings above it for bad weather and open seating for good weather.

After a short while, Bob and Ginnie came back to the table with their food.

"How is he doing?" asked Dusty, already feeling a great deal of responsibility for the boy.

"He's sleeping right now, but Andy did a great job getting him cleaned up and bandaged," said Ginnie.

"Yes, he's the best cook I ever hired, and that singing's great, too." added Bob.

Dusty laughed. "That's what Mike and I are waiting for, Uncle Bob."

"Yeah, Bob, bring it on." Mike added to the banter.

"We'll do that just as soon as we get dinner over and cleaned up," promised Uncle Bob.

As they sat finishing off their warm Dutch-oven peach cobbler, they heard the drone of an engine. The thwop, thwop, thwop of the blades piercing the evening sky as the helicopter made a slow circle around the camp.

"Jim, Hank, grab a couple of lanterns and set them out there so they can see where to put it down," Bob called out to his wranglers.

The two men grabbed lanterns, ran to the meadow, and set them on the ground to illuminate the flattest area for landing. The helicopter made a couple of slow passes, flashing its headlight on the ground. The last thing the pilot would want to do was land in a swamp. With the blades still thwopping after landing, three people jumped out; the pilot, a heavyset male paramedic, and slender female paramedic. They all appeared to be in their early 40s.

"Hi. We're from the airlift to safety program hired by your SPOT. My name is Steve," the heavyset man said. "Where is our patient?"

"Nice to meet you, Steve. I'm Bob Rose and this is my outfit. I'll take you to the patient. Just follow me."

The rescue team followed Bob into the tent, Steve carrying his medical bag with him. They weren't in there very long when they came out.

"You were right with the airlift," the heavyset man reported. "That's a pretty bad break and being outside for a couple of days hasn't helped it."

"Yes, that's what we figured," said Bob.

"Let me radio in and I can let you know which trauma center we'll head into," the pilot said.

"I think they're from the West Side of the mountains," offered Dusty.

"Well, that's good information, but it's not going to affect which trauma center we fly him to. Per insurance, we're bound to go to the closest one—even if it's only a matter of a few minutes," said the pilot.

"Okay. Good to know," said Bob. "This is the first opportunity I've had to use this thing since I bought it last year. Thank goodness!"

Ginnie talked to the pilot for a minute and then he went over and hopped into the cockpit of the small chopper. He walked back a few minutes later.

"Well, this is your lucky day. The nearest trauma center is going to be Harborview in Seattle. They are notifying search and rescue now." He walked toward the tent where the boy was lying.

"Good news. Thank you," said Ginnie.

"Well, for sure a lucky day for his mom, anyway," said Mike.

Dusty, Mike and Bob walked over to the tent to see if they could offer any assistance.

The heavyset paramedic stuck his head out. "Can we get some help with a makeshift carrier here, and we'll get him loaded into the helicopter."

They all linked hands, gently lifted the boy up, and walked him to the aircraft. The pilot cautioned them not to pull on anything on the helicopter. "Even though it looks like an ornament, everything on the outside and inside has a purpose, and I need it. So please don't tear it off."

"Well," said Dusty, "Our hands are kind of full right now, but we'll surely take that into consideration once we set Scott down."

"Ever the smartass, Boss," noted Mike, with an approving smile.

Scott looked like he was in a lot of pain. Dusty was glad that the boy didn't have to be tough anymore and he could rest. An occasional groan escaped from him. The pilot opened a door in the rear of the small craft and they carefully loaded him on a gurney and pushed it into the helicopter. Looking inside, Dusty thought it might have been a claustrophobic way to travel if you were feeling well, but for a person in and out of consciousness it was probably perfectly fine. All the instruments were inside the compartment so they could monitor Scott's vital signs and radio ahead to have treatment ready for his entry to the trauma center. Dusty felt much better after loading Scott into the helicopter.

The small encampment stood by as the pilot revved up the engine and took off, slowly circling the meadow with its spotlight shining in front. As soon as the craft gained altitude, it took off, leaving behind the moon and the mountain peaks silently around them.

"Wow," said Mike, "that was kind of like ET, or something, the way that thing blasted in and out of here. It feels like we imagined it."

"Yeah, the Pasayten never ceases to amaze me, Mike, but we didn't imagine anything. I'm getting up at first light and taking a look around Ramon Lake. I gave somebody my word and I plan on making good on it." Dusty pulled his hat off and ran his fingers through his hair.

"I'm with you, Boss."

"Well, that sounds like that's what needs to happen," said Uncle Bob. "But in the meantime, we've got dudes to entertain. What do you say we see if Andy can sing?"

"Let's do it," said Dusty. The men walked back to the campfire, Scout trotting at Dusty's heels.

"Now you're talking. That's what we've been waiting for," Mike grinned.

When they got there the singing had already begun. The dudes and Ginnie were clapping and laughing, Andy was quite the entertainer. They stayed for about an hour and then Dusty and Mike excused themselves. Catching and bridling their horses, they rode the short distance to Corral Lake in the moonlight.

Chapter Thirty-Four

Sally felt exhausted. Her pace was slowing down. Her clothes had long since dried out and they felt stiff and scratchy on her skin. She made her way out of the drainage and climbed through grassy meadows and small forested groves, avoiding open areas. Jumping off that waterfall, she should have lost them for sure, but she had a certainty in the pit of her stomach that she hadn't.

She went on, even slowly jogging when possible, keeping an eye out for a trail. Once she found one, she could follow nearby and use it as a guide.

The sun was dropping in the sky, and Sally's stomach growled again. She crouched by a stream, scooping water into her mouth and drinking thirstily. Giardia was the last thing on her mind at the moment. Now where were those huckleberries? There had been so many before, there had to be more. Sitting on a rock by the creek, she looked around. She would have to keep her eyes open as she walked.

Slowly she got up. The short rest had done little to curb her fatigue. She stretched her arms over her head, but immediately felt a stabbing pain in her shoulder and hip. She kept walking. After about half an hour she stumbled upon a well-worn trail. Her heart flip-flopped when she stepped onto it. Keeping an eye on the path, she kept going through the trees and brush on the far side. Before long she saw little red berries on the bushes.

At first eating was the most important thing, and she grabbed handfuls of the berries and stuffed them in her mouth. But after a few mouthfuls, she remembered the bear and cautiously looked around. Seeing nothing, she took a deep breath and her shoulders relaxed. She kept on eating. Before long, she felt full. Grabbing some more handfuls of berries, she put them in her pockets and kept walking.

The mountain peaks shone brightly in the late afternoon sun, and the air was beginning to take on a little chill. Sally's feet ached and her neck felt stiff. Between the jump into the waterfall and the tumultuous swim down the river, she marveled she was even alive. She felt a stab of worry about her dad and little brother. She would get out of here and find them, she resolved, if it was the last thing she did.

The rocks became silhouettes as the sky faded into a deep blue. Sally looked around for a place to spend the night. She climbed on top of a large boulder and lay down on its flat surface. From here she could see the trail, but no one could see her. She lay on her back and stared up at the sky. The stars were beginning to come out, and Sally did her best to find the North Star again like her dad had shown her. *Can Scott and Dad see it, too?* Sally had always liked the night sky. It was something she could share with people whether they were here or not. Sally pulled her shirt tightly around her. She felt less lonely and scared now. She smiled and fell into a light sleep on her rock.

Chapter Thirty-Five

Dusty woke up early. He hadn't slept very well, thinking about Scott and his family. He pulled on his jacket and hat, slipped into his Romeos, and went out the tent door. Scout followed. All four horses were still tied to the highline with their hobbles on. He unsnapped their leads, and they immediately put their heads down and began grazing, taking little steps to get to greener grass.

Dusty went over to the fire pit. He grabbed the ax and split the larger logs into thin pieces of kindling that would burn quickly. In no time at all a fire crackled. He grabbed the coffee pot and walked down to the lake. The sun had not yet come up and was just a faint glow in the east. The lake was still except for a few dips every so often as the trout fed on early morning bugs. Dusty felt an urgency to get going, but he breathed deeply of the cool mountain air laced with the scent of pine and fir. He was going to find Scott's family, but first things first. The horses had to eat so they would be ready for the trip. And he and Mike needed to get ready for the ride. He dipped the coffee pot into the clear water of the lake and watched the water swirl down into the pot. Dusty filled it up and dumped it out a couple of times to make sure it was fresh. On his final fill he took care not to take in any dirt or plants.

As he turned to head back up the hill to camp, he caught a slight movement out of the corner of his eye. A couple of deer had appeared near the trees by the lake. He stopped to watch. They were unaware of him as they carefully made their way down to the water's edge to drink. He stood still. The deer got their fill and then soundlessly walked back into the woods. Dusty looked at Scout who sat quietly, not missing a thing. "Good boy," Dusty patted his head. The most difficult thing Dusty had to do with Scout was train a herding dog not to herd. It was a necessity for mountain riding; there was just too much wildlife to have a dog chasing after it. It was also dangerous for the dog and his owner. You never knew who was going to come charging back out—a mother bear or elk protecting their young? Dusty mused as he set the coffee pot on the grill over the fire.

Mike was just coming out of his tent. "Wow, you beat me this time. What's going on, Boss?"

"I couldn't sleep very well; just kept thinking about Scott's family."

"Yeah, seeing a young boy like that all beat up physically and mentally really does grab you. I didn't sleep so well myself."

"The sooner we can get saddled up and get on the trail, the better."

They set about gathering their gear together and threw some hot water on for oatmeal while they waited for their horses to eat.

"Hey, Dusty, I heard animals can smell frying bacon for up to a mile away."

"Really? Well, maybe we can use that as the new replacement for dogs in hunting cougars."

"I guess we could try," agreed Mike, "I read that in a hunting magazine. This guy was frying bacon in his camper and he had a couple horses tied up outside. All of a sudden there was a big commotion and he had a cougar trying to take down his mare. Just about pulled over the camper."

"Well, that would be exciting."

"I expect it was, but it had a bad ending. The mare set back on her lead and pulled loose from the trailer. The last thing the guy saw was her back end running full bore into the forest with the cougar behind her."

"Sounds like that guy cooking bacon should have had a firearm close by," said Dusty.

"Maybe the story would have had a better ending that way."

They finished their breakfast and caught their horses to saddle up for the ride. They tied on their warm jackets and gloves in case they spent the night on the trail. Dusty checked to make sure his Ruger was loaded. Mike did the same. Dusty didn't relish the idea of shooting anyone, but the idea of being shot was even more distasteful. Anybody that would purposely ambush a family to abduct a young girl was up to no good. And if they were going to save her life, they needed to get there as soon as possible. The first 48 hours applied no matter where you were. Some people came into the backcountry thinking there were no laws. It would be up to him and Mike this time to remind them that there are.

As the men mounted up and rode out, the sun rose above the mountain peaks. They rode past Uncle Bob's camp and saw the fire burning with Andy outside cooking. Mike and Dusty waved and headed down the trail towards Ramon Lake. Andy held a cup of coffee up in a salute.

Chapter Thirty-Six

Cassie put her lunch in her saddlebags. "Are you about ready?"

"Yes, almost," said Terri. "You've got your fishing pole, right?"

"Already packed," said Cassie. "There is supposed to be really good fishing at Sheep Lake, and I haven't been there for a couple of years."

"Good, I can't wait!" Terri tied her fishing pole on behind her saddle.

Cassie put a baggie of horse treats in her saddlebag and a handful of dog snacks for Sammy. Despite the warmth of the morning, she tied her warm jacket and slicker on the back of her saddle. One never knew with the changeable weather of the high country. Her rifle was in the scabbard, and she was ready to go. Cassie mounted her big gray gelding Prince with one fluid motion.

Terri zipped up her tent and looked around. "That should be it. If I've forgotten anything, too bad." She untied her horse and brought him over to a log. "Boy, you are sure lucky you don't have to find anything to mount with. It would be so nice just to hop into the saddle. Whoa, Sugar." With a grunt, she mounted up.

"Well, there are shorter horses," laughed Cassie.

Terri affectionately straightened her horse's mane, "Shhh, don't let Sugar hear you say that. He'd be crushed."

The two packhorses highlined in camp whinnied as they rode out. There was always a ruckus when the horses were separated. It seemed it didn't take much at all for them to buddy up. Then when you took them apart, they acted like you were separating friends from birth. Cassie led up through the switchbacks out of the valley, heading back to the main trail they had ridden in the day before. Sammy trotted at her heels. In a very short time, they intersected the main trail and turned toward Sheep Lake.

"The trail is not actually marked, Terri; it's a user trail."

"Cool."

Cassie loved the no longer maintained trails in Washington. With the rainfall and moisture, sometimes the old bridges were rickety and dangerous, but the payoff was to see areas less traveled and left serene by riders of long ago. Their regular riding area of the Cascade Mountains held many such trails. All it took was a map and an adventurous spirit—Cassie and Terri had them both. To make it even better, their horses were mountain savvy with good stamina, so it was always a great adventure.

"Yeah, it really weeds out the crowds," agreed Cassie.

"Speaking of crowds," said Terri, "I haven't seen another soul up here since we passed that outfitter's camp at Crow Lake. Where is everybody?"

"That's my favorite part about this place; you don't see anybody. Or if you do, it's rare and you probably know them." She thought about the llama people and Dusty and Mike. She couldn't believe that they would be up here at exactly the same time and in the same area of the Pasayten. Washington was not exactly short on places to pack horses. Packer/lawyers, who would have thought? If the subject of her recreational pursuit ever came up, it was usually met with surprise and a complete lack of understanding. People either thought she hired someone to take her in, or she ran a pack outfit to be paid to take people in herself. It just showed how little people really understood the sport of horse packing. It certainly wasn't a new concept. Thank goodness for Back Country Horsemen where people could actually get together and share the hobby, Cassie mused.

"How long a ride is it over there?" asked Terri.

"Probably only about two hours. We'll see if we can come up

from the bottom on that old user trail, rather than ride all the way around. There is an old trail called Dead Horse Pass, but I think we'd be better off to come up it, rather than down. There used to be a big rock in the middle of the trail and it can be kind of tricky jumping down it with a straight drop-off in front of you.""By all means, let's take it on the way back," Terri quickly agreed.

"This weather is just beautiful, Cassie. Is it always like this?" The grass was a verdant green and the creeks flowed clear, the stones on the bottom glistening in the morning sun. Small purple flowers dotted the thick grass and gave off a sweet scent. Bunches of flowers resembling yellow daisies appeared intermittently around them.

"Don't even talk about the weather, I don't want to jinx it. It can change so fast up here it can make your head spin." Cassie adjusted her hat. "We have really been blessed so far, that's for sure. Maybe that weather station is accurate after all." She had Googled the Pasayten Wilderness and was able to get a reading for the wilderness itself. Weather reporting had come a long way. In the past she had had to rely on the nearest town, and that wasn't a lot of help. The Pasayten Wilderness had its own weather system, so even the closest town would not be accurate.

"Yeah, the thought of lightning was kind of scary. Glad that didn't happen—so far, anyway."

"So far so good, but you have to be ready for anything up here."

"Bring it on," joked Terri. And they rode down the trail as it followed the contours of the hillside. Another perfect day for a ride.

Chapter Thirty-Seven

Clem and Tom awoke on the ground in the trees. They had been following what they felt was the general direction Sally had taken the day before. Just when they were about to give up, they came upon the trail. And with the trail, they saw the boot prints of one person. One person with not very big feet.

Clem sat up and stretched. "Come on, Tom, we'd best git at it. The girl is not gonna be waitin' 'round for us all day."

Tom sat up. "Let's go." He stood and brushed his filthy clothes off, not that it made much of a difference. "When I get my hands on that little girl, I ain't never gonna let her go."

"Well, that's fer sure. She's a lot of work. Just let me git a little turn on her 'afore you do, I got a feeling there won't be much left." Clem guffawed.

"Boy, oh, boy, that's a fact." Tom rubbed his filthy hands together. "Let's git!"

The men walked out of the trees and followed the trail the same way Sally had gone.

Sally felt warmth on her face. The sun was so bright it burned as she opened her eyes and she rubbed them. Gravel crunched. She sat bolt upright. At first she thought it was her imagination, but then she was sure. Footsteps. Then voices.

"Clem, how far you figurin' she got?" Sally heard Tom's whiney voice.

Then Clem's raspy tone. "Cain't be that much further now. We're gainin' on her fer sure."

"You don't figure she ran into someone else up here, do ya?"

"Naw, not yet. But we gotta get her purty quick here."

Sally's heart stopped. She flattened herself in the center of her rock, pretty sure as long as she lay still and flat, they would not see her. The rock was at least 10 feet above the trail.

Sure enough, the two men walked by. Sally lay there for what seemed like an eternity, but she had to make sure that they were gone. Slowly she sat up and looked around. All looked clear. She heard the bees buzzing and the little creek nearby steadily trickled over the rocks. Other than that—nothing.

Crawling on her stomach, Sally inched over to the far side of the rock and let herself down. She peeked around the side of the rock, carefully looking up and down the trail. Again, nothing. Her heart began to slow to a regular beat as she relaxed. She dropped to the ground and crawled close to the granite wall of rock. Should she keep heading the direction she had been, which she figured was the trailhead, or go the opposite direction? It would make sense for them to keep going and not look back, so that would be a possibility. She made up her mind and took the first step when a grimy claw-like hand latched onto her shoulder.

"Clem, Clem, I got her," screeched Tom triumphantly. He grabbed her in a big bear hug from behind, and the rancid stench of his clothing and foul breath assaulted her nostrils.

Sally's insides froze with the touch of his hand on her shoulder. Then she went into an animal rage. She brought her elbow down hard and heard the sharp exhale of breath as she slammed into his diaphragm.

"You little bitch," he sputtered, fighting to keep ahold of her.

Sally stomped down as hard as she could on his foot, and Tom screamed, "Clem, git over here!"

Clem rushed over and punched her in the face. In her fight

mode the blow glanced off the side of her head, but hard enough that it stunned her.

Sally fought to keep conscious, but Tom quickly put her in a chokehold and everything went black as she fell to the ground.

"What a lil' hellcat," exclaimed Tom.

"That's fer sure," agreed Clem. "Help me tie 'er up afore she wakes up ag'in."

Tom, recovering from the scuffle, puffed up his chest. "Just think, if I hadn't had to take a leak, we would have walked away an' missed the whole thang."

"You did good. Now let's git 'er outta here afore anyone else comes along. Let's git back to camp, grab those horses and head to Sheep Lake."

"Let me jest get 'er tied up, so we ain't gonna have to chase her ag'in." Tom took one piece of rope and tied her hands together in front and the second piece of rope tied to one of her ankles, making a long line and then tying the other end to his belt. "She ain't goin' nowhere w'out me!"

Clem laughed. "Now that's smart thinking there, boy. Might be hope fer you after all." They headed cross-country back to their camp.

"How long you figger it's gonna be?" asked Tom.

"Not long. We can cut off a lot of the ground by just headin' straight through, probably get back there in an hour or so."

"Can't wait for Sheep Lake now," said Tom excitedly.

"Yeah, but you will wait this time. We cain't have the little boy showing up with anyone and ruinin' our fun ag'in. Sheep Lake ain't on the map as a reg'lar trail. We should be fine there. To do whatever we want." he added evilly.

"And that's just what I'm a fixin' to do." Tom laughed a low ugly laugh.

Sally froze inside. It was like she was in another world, a horror movie. How could they have found her? *Isn't this wilderness like a million acres?* Her stomach tightened and she felt nauseous. These weren't men, they were animals. She tried to clear her head. She had to escape, but how? Fear had not entered the picture yet, but disgust, revulsion and a bone-wearying sadness fell on her.

As Tom pushed her along from behind, she had to watch her feet to keep from falling face first. Sally's wrists were tied together. The rope that tied her ankle to Tom's belt kept tangling around her feet. It was all she could do to keep her balance and continue moving forward. Luckily, there was not much underbrush, mainly just grass to walk through. She felt hollow inside. Where were her dad and her brother? She could only hope that they were safe.

It seemed like hours, but they finally returned to the filthy tent and pack boxes piled nearby. Looking at the fire ring, Tom seemed to remember his face, still bruised by the log. "I outta take that log and bust you with it. See how you like it," he growled.

"We don't got no time fer that now, Tom. 'Sides you might kill her too soon," cautioned Clem. "I got some hot coffee to give her when we get set up at Sheep Lake. We just gotta move now."

"Yeah, yeah," Tom glared menacingly at Sally, "but the party up there is sounding like more fun all the time."

Sally made it a point to just stare straight ahead and not engage with either one of them. She didn't want to aggravate an already bad situation. She would just have to bide her time, but she would get out of here. She'd done it once, she'd do it again, she vowed. There was no question now what their end game was—they planned to kill her.

"Now that we got them boxes off'n old Rosie, let's just load the girl up on the horse," said Clem.

"That'll work."

"Much as I'd like to ride her with me, I don't think my horse can handle it."

"Yeah, them boxes almost done her in, but this girl's a lot lighter," said Tom.

They loaded up the last of their things on Clem's packhorse and then hoisted Sally on top.

With one last look around, Clem turned and headed down the trail to Sheep Lake, pulling Rosie and Sally behind him.

Chapter Thirty-Eight

The sun was well into the sky as they rode into the grassy bowl. Trees filled the bottom to their left and bare grassy hills to the right.

Clem studied the grass. "That trail's gotta be right around here." They rode one way and then doubled back.

Sally's head ached and her stomach was numb. The bony horse beneath her kept up a bone-jarring pace. Sweat dripped over her uneven tufts of hair dotted with bald spots. Sally felt a wave of sorrow for the horse and herself. She quickly brought herself back from it. No time to give a thought to anything but survival.

"Here it is," Clem said triumphantly. The trail appeared out of nowhere; a small dirt path winding down the hill through the grass and into the trees.

Clem led the way, followed by Sally, with Tom in the rear keeping a watchful eye. Once into the woods it was only a short distance before a cabin appeared on their left.

"Here we are." Clem reined in his horse.

The old one-room trapper's cabin stood back in a copse of trees. An old chopping block sat in the grass in front of the cabin, with a well-used fire pit surrounded by logs for seats. Old corrals in back appeared to have been patched and reinforced over the years.

"Let's get camp set up first an' then get to the fun," said Clem.

"What about havin' the fun first," whined Tom.

"We got nothin' but time after that, and I want to get some

coffee on." Clem, took a step towards Sally, glaring at her.

Sally looked straight ahead and didn't acknowledge him. They were not going to get the benefit of a reaction from her.

Tom walked up and pulled her roughly off Rosie. He dragged her, as she stumbled, to a tree and tied her up. Sally watched through veiled eyes as the men took the saddles off and led the horses over to a small creek a short distance away to water them. She could feel the warmth of the sun, but it did nothing to help the coldness she felt inside.

After putting the horses in the corral, Clem started a fire. "Tom, would you go git some water to start the coffee?"

Tom dug in the pack box and pulled out a fifth of whisky. "I bin saving this fer a special occasion. I think this is it." His face split in a huge gap-toothed grin.

"Now yer talkin'. Get that water fer the coffee and let's have us some drinks."

Tom took a big swig off the bottle and wiped his mouth with the back of his hand. He walked over and handed it to Clem.

Clem took a big swallow, his eyes watered and he belched loudly, "Mighty fine."

Turning back to the pack boxes, Tom dug out the coffee pot and headed to the stream. Sally watched as Clem pulled out his ax and laid it by the chopping block. He walked into the trees, picking up pieces of dead wood as he went. She fought off the feeling of dread as she tried to assess the situation. She had no idea where she was, other than deep in the wilderness. The rope this time was tight and it dug into her already burned flesh. She looked at the ax and knew she probably wouldn't get a chance to grab it. The cabin was remote, as was just about every place in the Pasayten. The odds of backpackers coming to Sheep Lake seemed impossible, especially since it appeared to be an unmarked trail. Despite her best efforts to repress them, tears streamed down her face. Thinking about her dad, Scott, and her mom waiting for all of them to come home was more than she could handle.

"Awww, look at her. The little hellcat is crying," mocked Tom as he set the coffee pot by the fire ring. He picked up the whisky bottle and took a big swig. He walked over and stood in front of her grinning. His scabby lips parted leaving a big gap with no front teeth and the ones he had left were coated yellow. Sally turned her head in revulsion.

A cloud of foul breath, soaked with whisky, blew over her, and Sally felt her stomach roil. As Tom reached out to touch her, she withdrew as far as the ropes would let her. He still managed to touch her arm and trailed his hand down her leg. She twisted away from him.

"Oh, little Miss Too Good for Everyone, huh? We'll see about that," Tom threatened, angry at the look on Sally's face.

"I think we got us a lil' rich girl here."

"Is that a fact? Wall, good. I've always wanted to have me one of those." Clem walked into the clearing with his arms loaded down with wood. "Hey, how 'bout helpin' me get this fire going? Plenty of time for that in a little bit."

"Do this, do that. When do we get to the good stuff, anyway?" Tom pouted as he stomped off.

"Jest get some wood. I want that coffee goin', then all time limits are off."

"Okay, okay." Tom headed into the trees, picking up some more downed wood. In a few minutes he came back with his arms full and dropped the load next to the fire ring.

Clem snapped some twigs and carefully laid them in a little pile. He lit a match and blew on the wood until a flame rose, then he carefully built the fire, putting on larger pieces. Tom sat by Clem on a log and watched, drinking from the bottle. Clem put the coffee pot on a rock next to the fire and stood up, surveying his work. "Ought to be boiling pretty soon. How's about 'nother drink of that hooch?"

Tom handed him the bottle. Clem took it and drank deeply. "Wall, what do you say we have a look-see here at what we got?"

"Now yer talkin'. Tom's filthy face broke into a big grin. He walked over to where Sally was tied. "Let's see what kind of tune Miss Too Good for Everyone Rich Girl sings now," he laughed a low ugly laugh.

Chapter Thirty-Nine

Dusty and Mike had been riding for a couple of hours, keeping their eyes on the trail for any sign of Scott's sister. When they came to a big flat rock, Dusty pulled up his horse and studied a group of prints. A narrow small set of hiking boots and then two large pairs of boots with pronounced heels. "Looks like a scuffle."

Mike leaned over to look. "I'd say this is a good chance of being them."

Scout stood by panting softly. "It is times like this, Scout, I really wish you were a bloodhound," Dusty said, only half teasing.

Scout cocked his head and gave him a lopsided grin with his tongue hanging out.

"So which way do you think these tracks are heading?" Mike squatted next to the prints.

"What do you want to bet Sheep Lake?" said Dusty. "That trapper's cabin nobody's supposed to know about—that everybody and their brother knows about."

The men headed down the trail.

It was early afternoon when they neared Sheep Lake.

"Hey, take a look at that." Mike pointed at the wisp of smoke rising above the trees to their left.

"Looks like we've got a campfire," said Dusty.

The trail petered out into a huge grass bowl with few trees and no lake visible. As the men cut across the field and picked up a small user trail, they heard a high pitched scream of terror from the trees below them.

Dusty spurred Muley and took off at a dead gallop with Mike and Scout right behind him. Reaching the trees, Dusty bailed off and hastily threw Muley's rope around a tree. He pulled his gun out of the holster and headed down to the cabin at a run. Mike was right behind him, gun drawn.

Tom grabbed Sally and roughly tossed her on the ground. "Wall, first things first. I feel like it's Christmas."

He grabbed Sally's shirt and ripped it down the front. She let out a horrified scream that bounced off all the peaks around them. He slapped her hard, and she fell to the ground. She covered her face with her hands and sobbed as if her heart would break.

"Looks like we're going to have to gag her. We cain't risk anyone hearin' her." Clem grabbed his sweaty handkerchief from his neck and tied it around Sally's mouth.

Never in her entire life had Sally encountered anything like this before. Her survival instincts were in overdrive, but what could she do? The gag tasted like stale sweat and body odor. She felt her gag reflex involuntarily kicking in. When that horrible man ripped her shirt, humiliation burned through her like a knife. Did he think she was so inconsequential that he could treat her like that? Her face ached. The last time he slapped her it felt like he had loosened a couple of her teeth. She lay on the ground praying for them to stop.

Tom stood over Sally and kicked her in the side. "Come on now, Honey, you can do better 'n this. You got to cooperate some. Guess we'll need to get a persuader."

He grabbed a thick tree branch. "What do you say we start out with a little spankin'," he said with a nasty laugh. He rolled her over with a kick and raised the stick over his head. As he got ready to bring it down, a shot rang out. Tom dropped the stick, staggered backwards and grabbed his shoulder.

"What in the hell?" Blood spurted through his fingers and his face went white.

Clem dropped to the ground and belly-crawled to his saddlebags. As he grabbed his gun, a tall man in a cowboy hat walked out of the trees pointing a Ruger Vacquero handgun at him. "Drop it."

As Sally watched in horror, Clem seemed to think over his options for a second, but then a second man with a gun drawn appeared behind the cowboy. A dog standing by the men growled low in his throat.

Clem spread his hands, palms up. "Well, hey, fellas, I think you got us all wrong here. Just keep yer damn dog off'n me. We was just planning on having us a little party and this here girl is all in with us on it. Ain't that right, Honey?"

Sally shook her head violently from side to side. Keeping one eye on Tom, the olive-skinned man walked over and pulled the gag out of her mouth. She sputtered and spat out the vile taste from the sweaty rag. "That's a lie! Please, let me go! These men kidnapped me!"

"That's exactly what we're here to do, Sally. I'm Dusty. Your brother sent us," said the tall man.

"Scott is okay?" A weight seemed to lift from Sally's chest. "Could you please untie me?"

"My pleasure. Mike, could you cover me?" The man called Dusty pulled his pocket knife out of his belt.

"You bet, Boss."

Dusty knelt down and cut through the ropes on Sally's hands and ankles. "We'll get you some cream for those rope burns as soon as we can."

"Thanks." She quickly rubbed her wrists and modestly held her shirt together as best she could with all the buttons torn off. Relief poured through her body and tears ran down her face.

The dog trotted over, nuzzled her hand and sat next to her. Sally hugged him and patted his furry head.

"What about my Partner, here?" demanded Clem. "Look what you done to him! He needs a doctor."

"That's pretty far from his heart, I'd say. What do you think, Mike?"

"I'd say he's going to live."

"Our main concern here is getting this little girl back with her family and, of course, turning you guys into the law," said Dusty. "Let's get them tied up."

"Where's my dad and brother?" asked Sally.

Dusty turned to her. "Sally, we haven't found your dad yet. Your brother had a broken arm and a pretty good fever. We got him airlifted out last night and I'm sure he's with your mom now."

"What about my dad?"

"Once we get you safe, we're going to find him. I'm sure he'd want you kids taken care of first. Us dads are just wired that way."

"Okay." Relief flooded through Sally.

"Let's take care of these guys, Mike, and then let's hit the trail."

"Right, Boss." Mike ripped Tom's shirt and made a makeshift bandage over the gunshot wound in his arm. "You're just going to have to wait to get that removed. It ought to be okay."

"But I'm shot. I could bleed to death," Tom whined. "Help me!"

"I am helping you, which is a whole lot more than I feel like doing right now." Mike got Tom loaded up in his saddle with his shoulder in a sling and his feet tied underneath his horse's belly.

"Don't be trying anything funny, either," warned Dusty. "I'd hate to have to give you a matched set."

Tom just glared at him.

Digging in his saddlebags, Mike came up with a new roll of nylon rope and handed it over to Dusty.

After Clem was mounted on his horse, Dusty tied Clem's hands in front of him with a series of half-hitches on the slippery rope and pulled it tight—hoping that would stop it from stretching. New rope could be a pain, but you had to use what you had in the mountains.

"Ow," complained Clem, "Yer cuttin' off my circulation."

"I think you'll live." Dusty pulled the bridle off Clem's horse. "You won't be needing this." He put the bridle into his saddle bag. Not that it was worth keeping, ratty thing that it was, but he was going to pack it out regardless.

Dusty untied his coat from the back of his saddle and handed it to Sally. "You can wear this until we can find you another shirt."

"Thank you." Sally accepted the coat gratefully. Dusty helped her slip it on. It was a lined jean jacket and it smelled like campfire smoke with a faint hint of aftershave. She finally felt safe for the first time in days.

Chapter Forty

Clem was biding his time. He still had his cheater gun in his pants leg, and he just needed to wait until the time was right to make a move. There was no way they were going to take him out of here alive. He and Tom had met in prison and they had made a pact not to go back there.

Dusty mounted Muley and pulled Sally up behind him. For the second time in as many days, Muley carried two riders.

"You have a nice horse, Mister," said Sally, admiring Muley's strong flanks as they began walking.

"Why, thank you. By the way, my name's Dusty. Might as well call me that since we'll be riding together for a while here. And my friend over there is Mike."

"Okay, Dusty," said Sally. "So Scott looked like he was going to be okay?"

"Yes, he did. He had been out for a few days and had gotten a little banged up. His arm looked like it was broken, but other than that he looked just fine," said Dusty.

Sally felt comforted when she heard Scott was rescued. She still had icy dread in the pit of her stomach when she thought about her dad out there, but at least she knew that Scott was going to be okay.

"Looks like you've had a rough time yourself," said Dusty.

Sally didn't answer right away, thinking about sleeping outside, eating berries, the bear, the waterfall, the horrible men. "Yes," she finally managed as tears welled up in her eyes, "it has been a pretty rough time."

The line of horses went out with Dusty and Sally in the front, followed by Tom on his horse and Clem on his, and Mike took up the rear, his gun drawn. They followed the regular trail. This was not a good time for adrenaline trails like the Dead Horse Pass; it was enough trying to keep track of everyone and making sure Tom and Clem didn't pull any fast ones. They rode in silence through the grassy meadow and then down through the trees in the drainage on the user trail. It was rocky, but pretty easy to follow.

They had been riding for about an hour when Clem said, "I gotta take a leak."

Dusty reined in Muley. "Okay, but do it nice and slow. We don't want to lose anybody."

Clem had managed to work his hands just about free under the nylon ropes. His constant pulling had finally paid off and the rope had stretched. He made a big show of uncomfortably grabbing the saddle horn and then swinging himself to the ground, holding his hands together. He walked a couple of steps and then pretended he was relieving himself. He swore like something had bit him in the leg and he bent down to scratch it.

Dusty gazed into the distance, thinking about Sally and how tough this had been for her and her family. He mused about the fact that you just never really knew what would happen next in the backcountry. Right when you think you got it all figured out, something totally unexpected happened, be it weather, people, animals, whatever.

"You'd best hand down the girl again." Clem's raspy voice jolted Dusty back into the present. He smiled a yellow broken-toothed grin and pointed a gun at Dusty.

"I wouldn't bet on that so fast," said Mike, pointing his gun at Clem.

"Wall, you may think you can take me out, but I'm goin' t' take someone with me first," Clem wheezed. "I'm thinkin' it might have to be this purty little thing." He gestured his gun at the girl.

"Plug that girl, Clem," agreed Tom. "She's caused us 'nuff trouble now."

Sally froze with fear again. *Unbelievable.* Every time she thought she would finally be okay…she wasn't.

"Just hold on there a minute," said Mike. "You don't need to be shooting anybody."

Dusty tried to think. They couldn't let them have Sally again. If the men took her this time, they'd kill her. If they stood them off, someone was going to get hurt.

Sally was already moving. "Don't shoot anyone. I'll come." Before Dusty had a chance to grab her, she slid off Muley. Traumatized, she knew she couldn't stand for anyone else to be shot. She mechanically walked over to Clem.

"Now, that's more like it. Come on, Tom."

"I will, as soon as you come untie me."

Clem grabbed the girl and pushed her in front of him toward Tom. He raised his foot to kick her down the trail. The split second Dusty reached for his gun, the roar of a rifle split the air. Clem stopped right where he was, stood for about a half second with a shocked expression on his face, and then dropped in his tracks. Face first into the dirt. Dusty looked around stunned. He hadn't fired his gun.

Tom began yelling frantically from his horse, "Clem! Clem! What in the hell are ya doin'? Git up! Git up!"

Clem would not be getting up again. The top of his head was gone.

As everybody stared down at the inert form in shock, Cassie walked in, holding her rifle. "Is everyone okay?"

"Where did you come from? How in the hell did you

do that?" Dusty sputtered in amazement.

"It was actually pretty easy. I just aimed and pulled the trigger," Cassie said calmly. "It appeared to be a pretty bad situation. I've been watching for a while. Terri is holding our horses down at the main trail. We heard shots and screaming early on, so I came to have a look myself. After watching this guy here, it didn't appear there was much else to do with him," she added. "Putting him down was not my first choice, but it appeared to be his."

Chapter Forty-One

"Is everybody else okay?" Cassie asked again.

Sally stood white as a sheet, staring at Clem. She felt comforted that he was no longer a threat, but seeing him dead was a shock. She had never seen a dead person before, and it seemed surreal. The only saving grace was her gut instinct, knowing if it wasn't him lying there, it would have been her.

Tom, still sitting on the horse, cried softly. "Clem didn't do nothin'. You had no call to do that."

Mike slid off his horse, "Cassie, thank you very much for your help. It came at a very good time."

Dusty was still speechless. This woman could not only ride a horse, she could shoot a gun, and she was beautiful and strong. He finally came around, dismounted, and walked over to the girl who stood staring at Clem.

"Come on, Sally. Come over here and sit down for a couple of minutes while I help these guys. Everything is going to be okay now." Dusty put his arm around her shoulders and led her over to sit down by a tree. Then he walked over to the others.

Cassie and Mike were getting Clem ready to pack out. "Have you got a tarp with you?" said Cassie.

"I've got one tied around my slicker. Hang on just a second." Mike brought the tarp and laid it out on the ground.

176

Dusty watched Cassie as she swung her long light-brown hair back and bent down to grab Clem's feet. She and Mike laid him out in the middle of the tarp. Brain matter and bone oozed from the wound on top of his head. From where he stood, Dusty could see the corpse's eyes were fixed and glassy, never seeming to move off them as they worked. His broken yellow teeth gaped in a grotesque look of surprise.

Mike pulled Clem's shirt off and tied it around his head to staunch the flow of material oozing out and to cover his face. They all three grabbed a side of the tarp and rolled the body up in it. Using some more of Mike's nylon rope, they tied the bundle and they loaded him over the top of his horse. The bony little horse jumped back as they started to put the body on, but then he apparently resigned himself to the load. Dusty and Mike tied Clem's hands to his feet under the horse so he wouldn't flop around.

Dusty could not believe the matter-of-fact way Cassie went about dispatching Clem's body. He was in a combination of shock and awe. Finally he found his voice. "Thank you, Cassie. We couldn't have done it without you. You are one able woman."

"My pleasure, Dusty. Always glad to help out when I can." She blushed at the appraisal. "I guess years of hunting camp finally paid off."

"Cassie, I learned one thing today: I don't ever want to piss you off!" said Mike.

Cassie smiled. "Yeah, I guess you don't."

They all laughed uneasily, mounted up and went down the trail. The horror of what almost happened to the girl, coupled with the violent death of Clem was a lot to digest, and no one spoke on the ride back to camp.

Cassie led the way on foot, images of the scene running through her mind like a slide show. Once it had become a hostage situation, she'd had to break it. She could not risk harm to the girl. The only choice she had was to wait for a clear shot and then take it.

Killing a person disturbed Cassie. She repressed her misery at taking a life and instead focused on what she needed to do. She and Terri were going to have to pack out tomorrow, head into Winthrop, and file a police report.

Putting in her dues as a young prosecutor had helped with part of it. When she had started out in the law, she had not been an advocate of the death penalty. But after witnessing the prison revolving-door system, and seeing so many released convicts committing crimes more heinous than the last, she got a new attitude about mankind. There were some people that were just better off out of the picture. They would never be able to stop themselves from harming others.

The whole incident had played out pretty quickly, but with every bone in her body, she knew this was one of those men. All of her protective instincts came on full force when she saw the vile way he treated the young girl. Saving her was more important than saving him. She walked robotically, numbly putting down one foot and the other. She had filled her deer tag every year, but killing an animal for meat was not a comparison to the human wreckage they had just rolled up and tied on the packhorse.

She could still feel the pressure on her trigger finger. Bile rose in her throat. She was going to have a lot to deal with mentally and legally, but now was not the time to think about it.

Cassie took a deep breath to clear her head, suddenly aware of Dusty behind her, He seemed really good with kids, carefully carrying the young girl behind him. Bundled up in the oversized jean jacket, dirty blonde hair streaming down her back, the girl had her arms around Dusty's waist. Her head was resting on his back, appearing to be dozing off. Cassie saw the trust in the girl's relaxed face. She admired that a lot. If kids and animals trusted him, he must be a good guy. Thinking about him in a courtroom was so far removed from where they were now. He seemed like a different person.

Dusty watched Cassie's long legs as she strode down the uneven rock trail. Her hair cascaded down her back under her cowboy hat. She was slim, but athletic in her step. He had to admit she was a very attractive woman. He shook his head. It seemed like a crazy thing to be thinking, especially right now, but that's what he was thinking. It was a whole lot better than dwelling on their cargo.

They finally intersected the main trail where Terri sat with her arms around Sammy and the two horses tied to trees.

"I heard the shot. What happened? Is everyone all right?" Running over to the young girl seated behind Dusty she asked, "Are you okay?"

"I think so," answered Sally. Shock and tiredness appeared to have taken their toll. The young girl was leaning against Dusty with her eyes half closed.

"Cassie, what happened?" Terri tried again. "Sammy was going nuts. It was all I could do to hold him!"

"Those men kidnapped this girl and had Dusty and Mike at gunpoint. I came along at a good time to help them," said Cassie.

"She sure did," said Dusty with a big smile.

"I'll second that," said Mike.

Dusty reined Muley to the trail, "Well, let's get back to Uncle Bob's. I'm sure they're wondering what happened to us."

Cassie easily swung into the saddle and gathered up her reins. Terri moved her horse next to a rock, got on, and they all headed out. Sammy followed on the heels of Cassie's gray gelding.

Cassie looked expectantly at Dusty, waiting to see who wanted to go in front down the trail.

"Oh, by all means, ladies first." He gestured down the trail.

Cassie's mouth turned up with a faint trace of a smile as she reined her horse to lead the group.

"You're such a gentleman, Dusty." Terri fell in behind Cassie. Dusty smiled a shy boyish smile, and Terri laughed.

The group rode down the grassy trail through the mountains. Tom slouched dejectedly in his saddle, hands and feet securely tied. This time Mike had checked for anymore weapons. He continued to ride with one hand on his gun. Nobody wanted a repeat of the last catastrophe. Clem's horse trotted along behind with its load.

Cassie's horse kept a good pace. The sun was dropping lower in the sky, and they wanted to make Crow Lake by dinnertime. She figured she and Terri better drop in and see if they'd heard anything more about Sally's dad.

Even though he was two horses behind her, she was keenly aware of Dusty's presence. Different thoughts ran through her mind. Her grandpa, an old farmer in a little town called Toledo, would have said, "Some people just need killing. They're just no good." Cassie knew she had just made the world a better place.

"Cassie," Terri called out behind her.

"What?"

"Isn't this crazy? This is my very first pack trip into the Pasayten and look at what's happened. A kidnapping. A dead guy. And I thought just loading my horse up and staying in the woods was going to be the big thing."

"I do have to admit, this is the first time anything like this has happened to me on a pack trip, and I've been coming up here for more than 20 years," Cassie said, smoothing Prince's mane.

Dusty joined in the conversation. "The craziest thing that has ever happened to me up here to this point has been with a bear. I would have never believed anything like this could happen in the wilderness. Just kind of shows what things are coming to in the world."

Shooting a man was not something Dusty had had to do before, either, but when he saw Tom attacking the young girl, stopping it was a gut reaction. He knew he would have to fill out a statement about his part in what happened, as well as Cassie. Still, he did what he needed to do. Tom wasn't dead. The back of Dusty's neck tightened as he thought about the wreckage and pain these animals brought to Sally and Scott. *The rat deserved to be dead.* It was quiet as everybody rode, deep in their own thoughts, processing what had happened and letting the mountains, trees and flowers around them help with the healing process.

Chapter Forty-Two

Cassie saw the smoke from the campfire long before they got to the camp. As they rounded the last hill they looked down on the activity at Crow Lake. Along with the dudes, search and rescue people had arrived. A handful of dome tents were set up around the edge of the meadow and people were milling about in small groups.

As they wound their way into camp, Uncle Bob hurried up with the search and rescue people following him.

"You've got the girl," he exclaimed with a huge grin.

"Yes, we do," Dusty replied. "Come on over here, Uncle Bob, and I'll hand her down to you."

Bob stepped next to Muley to help Sally dismount. Still groggy from shock, dehydration and lack of sleep, she was hanging onto Dusty. When Bob came up, he caught her just as she began to slide off.

"Hey, Sally, so glad to see you." Bob looked concerned. "Looks like you'll be needing some rest and food. Lucky for you we've got the best camp cook in the Pasayten Wilderness."

Sally managed a slight smile. She croaked out, "Where's my dad?"

Bob's smile faded. "We haven't located him yet, but we've got a full party of search and rescue here now. Some of them arrived early afternoon and took off toward Ramon Lake already. Another group just arrived a few minutes ago, and they are putting together a plan to scour the countryside. Don't worry about your dad; we'll find him."

Cassie dismounted and handed the reins to Terri. "Hi, I'm Cassie Martin." She held out a hand to Bob. "I can help Sally while you deal with the rest of the cargo, if you'd like."

Bob stopped, and for the first time looked at the rest of the horses. He saw Mike with his gun out, one man bleeding and tied on his bony horse. And finally, his eyes went to the large bundle tied over the top of the scrawny animal ponied by Mike.

"Hi, Cassie. Bob Rose." He handed her Sally. "Go ahead and take her up to the fire. Andy will get her fixed up right away."

Cassie put an arm around Sally and the two of them walked to the fire.

Bob, clearly amazed, said, "Well, I'll be damned. I've heard of this stuff up here, but I've got to say in the 35 years I've spent in this wilderness, this is the first time I've witnessed anything like this!"

Bob scratched his head and called to his wranglers, "Hank, Jim, can you help the boys with their loads over here?"

"One of them doesn't need much help," said Dusty.

"I can see that now. Well, I guess we'll just roll him off to the side and wait for the airlift."

Tom was coming back to life with the new audience and began to whine in earnest, "They kilt my frind in col' blood. He didn't have a chance."

"Just relax. You'll have plenty of time to talk about it later," said Mike.

Bob grabbed Tom's horse's rope. "What do you say you put the cargo down by the horses and keep this guy down there, too? I am still trying to run a dude operation here."

"Hand me your lead rope. I'll pull your packhorse and escort this one down by the horses, which, in my opinion, is too good for him," said Jim.

Mike and Dusty went down to the corrals with the wranglers and unloaded the men.

"Hopefully Uncle Bob has notified the airlift and sheriff to get everybody out of here. I imagine they will deal with the Border Patrol."

"The sooner the better. They haven't allowed trash in these woods for a long time; you always got to pack it out. You know, leave no trace," said Mike.

They tied the thin horses up and hobbled their own out. "I hate to tie these animals up," said Dusty gloomily, "but who knows what kind of diseases they've got. I'd say by looking at them the least would be worms and lice. We can put them out once all of ours have eaten."

"Seeing animals treated like that makes me sick," Mike said ruefully. "Hopefully we can get them in with an animal rescue group."

Jim and Hank helped hold Tom as Dusty and Mike tied him securely to a tree.

"You don't need ta be treatin' me this way," he begged. "I'm hurt. My shoulder is all shot up."

"And I'd hate to see what the little girl up there would look like now if your shoulder wasn't shot," Mike said with disgust.

Dusty's face was implacable and he agreed, "Ain't that the truth? Let's head up to the fire and see what Andy's got cooking. What do you say, boys?"

The four men left Tom pleading at the tree and walked up to the camp.

Chapter Forty-Three

As he walked into the fire area, Dusty was greeted by a booming voice. "Well, look here, Dusty. Me, Brighty and Boss just couldn't wait anymore. We decided to see if Bob would be a needin' help up here ourselves!"

"Well, if it isn't Gold Dust Charlie." Dusty smiled. He barely got the words out when the larger man engulfed him in a bear hug.

"Looks like we come at the right time, too. This place is downright busy."

"Yes, you did. Mike and I were just on a little pack trip, stopped by to see Uncle Bob, and right after that things just seemed to get real complicated."

"Yes, so I heard. Well, glad to be of service in any way I can."

"We were going to get some dinner and see what Uncle Bob needs us to do. Our horses are hobbled out right now, but at some point we need to head back to our own camp next door at Corral Lake and get some sleep."

As Dusty talked, he let his eyes drift, and they seemed to find their target like a magnet. Cassie sat on a log by the fire with Terri. Excited, Terri chatted to the dudes while Cassie stared into the fire in contemplation. Dusty was worried about Cassie. He couldn't keep himself from glancing over at her. Shooting somebody, even in self-defense, was a tough thing to process. Without hearing what

Charlie had said, he finished the conversation and walked over to Cassie. "Mind if I sit down?"

"Not at all. Help yourself." She smiled faintly.

"Where's Sally?"

"Andy took her and gave her some stew. She kept insisting that she wasn't tired, but he got her to lie down in his tent, and she was out like a light."

"The rest will probably do her good until they get an airlift in here."

"Yes, I'm sure it will."

"So what are your plans now?" asked Dusty.

"I was talking to Terri, and this changes our pack trip entirely. We are going to have to go back over to our camp tonight at Peevy Pass, pack up tomorrow and head out. I have to file a report with the sheriff's office. I've never done it before, but I'm pretty sure you need to at least let law enforcement know why you've shot someone."

"Makes sense to me. I've never shot anyone before, either, although I can't say there haven't been situations in which I wish I could have." Dusty tried to make a joke of it.

Cassie managed a tired smile. "Well, amen to that. I guess now I'm living the dream."

"I'll be needing to make a statement, as well, but I want to help find the kids' dad first." Dusty shifted in his seat in front of the fire. He could feel the long ride in his back and legs. The heat from the fire felt good.

"Well, I wanted to say thank you again. I can't imagine how it would have turned out had you not come along when you did. Things just came unwound in a big hurry, and the more I think about it, the more I just don't know what we would have done." Dusty stared into the fire and replayed the day's events in his mind, acutely aware of the beautiful woman beside him, and the part she had played.

Cassie felt bone tired and staring into the fire she felt her muscles relax. The deep timbre of Dusty's voice and his closeness in proximity she found comforting. She had so many emotions running through her—happiness that the young girl was okay, relief that she had actually been able to react under extreme pressure of the moment, and at the same time she was appalled at the outcome. She knew she would work through it and be okay—it was a scenario she had run through her mind ever since she began shooting firearms. Cassie still heard her shooting instructor's voice in her head: *Don't wear a sidearm unless you are prepared to use it.* Well, that part wasn't an issue anymore. She took a sip of coffee and just listened to the buzz around her.

Terri bubbled as she filled in the dudes on her first pack trip in the Pasayten. Her cheeks were pink and hand gestures wild. Packhorses, mountain rescues, and bad guys—she wasn't sure that she would ever be able to top it. Everyone tried to steer clear of discussing the wrapped-up load next to the horses and the man tied to the tree.

Dusty stole one more look at Cassie. Sipping a cup of coffee, her cheeks flushed from the fire and exhaustion. She was beautiful, no doubt. *What in the hell is wrong with me?* He scolded himself. "Well, I better see what Uncle Bob has in store for me now." He stood up, eager to get away and at the same time not wanting to leave. Cassie looked up at him with sad light-blue eyes.

"Take care, Dusty." She turned back to the fire.

"You, too." Dusty had never noticed that before, light blue like the summer sky. He shook his head quickly and walked away.

Cassie kept staring into the fire and nodded.

As Dusty approached, Bob was just giving instructions to his hands. "I got ahold of the sheriff's office by satellite phone. They will be sending in a special helicopter to evacuate the prisoners. I told them the sooner we got them out of here, the better for everyone involved. They ought to be here in an hour or so, and they are going to land out in the meadow where we had our emergency airlift for the boy."

"What about the girl, Sally?" Dusty asked, looking at Uncle Bob with concern, a paternal instinct kicking in.

"I told them that she wasn't critically hurt, so she didn't need a Medevac, but she does have one hysterical mother who has been calling repeatedly for her daughter's rescue. In light of that, they feel it's in everyone's best interest to evacuate the girl, as well," Bob answered.

"Well, that's probably best, anyway. If her dad's critically injured or dead, her mother should be with her," agreed Dusty.

Bob nodded and turned to his wranglers. "Jim, Hank, could you please head out there and place some lanterns to mark the landing area. It's getting dark pretty fast and we want them to be able to land as easily as possible."

"Yes, Boss," they both answered. The two men headed toward the mess tent in search of lanterns.

"This is the most excitement I've ever had up here. Hope I still have a dude string left when it's over." Bob pushed his hat back and wiped his forehead with one hand.

"I don't know. I think the dudes are pretty much entertained with it all." Dusty turned to look at the campfire as a deep raucous laugh sounded, followed by the higher-pitched sound of the dudes joining in.

"Gold Dust is going to have them laughing so hard they are going to think this whole little side show is part of the trip," said Dusty.

"That man has certainly got the gift of gab, and I've missed him," agreed Bob. "He couldn't have come at a better time."

Andy banged on his Dutch oven with a spoon. "Dinner is served, you lucky people. Come and get it before I throw it out!"

The family got up from the fire, followed by Cassie, Terri and Gold Dust Charlie. Everybody filed by the green checkered tableclothed table. The plates and silverware were laid out. They helped themselves to fruit salad and rolls. Andy stood by the big

Dutch-oven pot and ladled out stew into bowls.

"Don't get too full. We got Dutch Oven Blueberry Buckle for desert. One of my specialties, if I don't say so myself." He looked down at the ground smiling in feigned modesty.

"Well, come on, Dusty. Let's get some grub before he throws it out." Bob laughed and slapped Dusty on the back.

Chapter Forty-Four

They were all sitting around the fire finishing up their Blueberry Buckle when the thwop, thwop, thwop sounded. Everybody looked over at the field as the sheriff's helicopter touched down.

"This is getting to be a regular airport." Bob stood, set down his empty bowl, and headed out to meet the undersheriff.

Dusty and Mike were close behind. Bob's hired hands were back down with the prisoner.

Cassie stood up, "Well, we better hit the trail so we can get back to our camp within some reasonable amount of time. Thank you so much for the great food, Andy."

"Yes, thanks, Andy. It was all so good. I'm ready to take a nap now." Terri winked at him.

Cassie put her hands on her hips in a mock reprimand. "No naps until we get back!"

The dudes all said good-bye. Gold Dust gave them each a big bear hug.

"Please make sure and tell Bob thank you for all of his hospitality," said Cassie.

"No problem. I will relay the message," said Andy. "Sorry to see you go."

"Yes, it would be nice to be a little closer, but we have got to get everything packed up and out tomorrow," said Cassie.

The women walked over to their horses, tightened the cinches and put their bridles on. Mounting up, they rode out, leaving the bustle of the men, and the helicopter, and the warm fire burning behind them. Sammy followed behind them.

"What a day!" said Cassie.

"Yeah, I'm sorry to see my first pack trip in the Pasayten come to a close so quickly."

"Well, don't worry. You've done really well. We'll be back."

"Oh, boy, I was hoping you would say that!"

Cassie thought ruefully, Y*es, only a few small things to get taken care of first*. She checked her rifle absently as she rode along. The sky was turning dark gray to black with no stars out. That was not a good sign. So far the unpredictable Pasayten weather had been really good, but that could change without any warning. The way the day had gone so far, Cassie was really hoping at least the Google weather search would be right.

Dusty helped get the prisoners on the helicopter. When he came back to get Sally, she was sound asleep. He hated to wake her up after all she had been through. As he picked her up and carried her out, she barely moved. She didn't weigh anything. She reminded him a lot of his own daughter when she was young.

A couple of sheriff's deputies had come in on the flight, knowing they were going to have to watch the prisoner and keep the girl safe at the same time. Dusty handed her carefully over to the deputy. He took her inside the cockpit and Dusty stepped back. The blades were already rotating for take-off. "We've got to beat feet out of here, not a minute to spare. Just heard they are expecting some weather in tonight," the pilot announced.

Dusty grimaced. *That's just great. The perfect end to this day.*

He and Mike watched as the helicopter lifted off. With the big spotlight shining on the ground, it did a quick sweep of the meadow and flew out of sight. The clouds swirled around the peaks, and the sky was dark and starless.

He and Mike walked back to the campfire. The first thing Dusty noticed was, she was gone!

"Where is Cassie?" he couldn't help but ask.

Gold Dust Charlie said, "Well, her and her friend figured they better head out, seeing's they had a long ways to go. And don'tcha worry yourself none, Dusty. I gave 'em both a big hug for you." He looked pleased with himself.

"Well, thanks for that." Dusty gave him a smile, even though he really didn't feel much like smiling.

Mike stretched. "Well, another day, another trail. Speaking of that, we might as well get back, too. We got horses to hobble out still."

"Yeah, I guess so."

"Well, I mean now that the women and excitement are over." He poked Dusty in the side.

Dusty shot him an amused look, and they went to collect their horses.

Once mounted they made a final ride through the camp.

"Thanks a lot, Uncle Bob, Andy. Great seeing you, Gold Dust, and the rest of you folks. We'll be back by tomorrow on our way to look for the missing man."

Bob walked up from the fire. "My pleasure, as always, Dusty. You boys get some rest, and we'll see you bright and early in the morning."

"Good night all," said Mike. The two men rode into the dark night, Scout trotting behind.

As they approached their camp, welcoming neighs sounded and were returned by Dusty and Mike's horses.

They made quick work of stripping the saddles, hobbling their horses, and turning them all loose to graze.

After building a small campfire, they did their best to stay awake until the horses had eaten.

Chapter Forty-Five

A sharp crack sounded overhead and Dusty awoke with a start. He sat bolt upright, heart pounding, waiting for the tent to be struck down right on top of him. Only a couple of seconds more and a huge boom sounded.

The pilot was right, thunder and lightning. Scout whimpered and moved closer to him. "I know how you feel. Boy, I hate it, too."

The next crack that sounded, Dusty counted, "One thousand one, one thousand two, one thousand three"—boom.

"Oh, man, that's pretty close, Scout."

How on earth is a man supposed to sleep when he is in danger of becoming roasted alive by lightning? Dusty checked his watch, 3 o'clock. Why was it always something like 3 o'clock in the morning when this stuff happened? It wasn't like you could get up and do something else. No, you were just stuck with it. He sighed and wondered how Sally was doing. She was for sure reunited with her mother and brother by now. That was probably a bittersweet reunion.

The sheriff's office would have gotten Tom and Clem delivered to their respective places. Tom to jail and Clem to the Medical Examiner's office. Now that it was over, Dusty had time to think about it. It really bothered him. He felt violated. The irreverence and disrespect stabbed him in the gut. There was no way around it. The wilderness had always been his sanctuary, and the Pasayten

Wilderness above all had been sacred to him. People like Clem and Tom never had any interest in being in the backcountry. It made a person really think twice about going into the wilderness now. Roughing it was one thing, survival was another. If the border was getting as bad as he kept hearing, he may have to do some pack trips farther in the interior of the United States. What about Uncle Bob, though? He had a permit up here; it was his livelihood. They would have to do some research with the Border Patrol and sheriff's office now to see just how bad this had become.

As Dusty thought more about the day, an image came to mind of a woman with long light-brown hair and mountain-sky-blue eyes riding away on a silver horse. He wondered how she felt after dispatching Clem. It had to be tough. Seeing the young girl had probably really helped. At least he hoped it did...

"Dusty?" a voice called from the other tent.

"Yeah?"

"Do you think we're gonna get fried?"

"I hope not. We need to go on a manhunt tomorrow."

"Man, I hate this crap!"

"Me, too!"

Another lightning flash and then a boom almost immediately.

"Don't think it could get any closer. It's right overhead," said Dusty.

"Great."

The storm continued, and a torrential rain pounded their tents. Finally, after what seemed like hours, the thunder and lightning quit, and Dusty was able to sleep.

Chapter Forty-Six

Cassie and Terri were both dead tired when they came into camp. They stripped the saddles off, hobbled their riding stock and then turned the highlined packhorses loose to graze.

"You think about an hour will be enough?" said Terri.

"It's got to be. I don't think I can stay awake any longer than that, can you?"

"No, that's why I was asking."

"Let's build a little fire while we're waiting and put some coffee on."

"Good idea."

The women sat around the fire drinking their coffee and thinking about their day. With all the search and rescue already out there, they would have plenty of manpower to find the girl's father.

The fire radiated warmth against the chilly night air. Cassie pulled her coat a little tighter around her.

Terri poked the fire with a stick. "Those were sure a bunch of nice people at the outfit."

"Yeah, they were."

Terri sighed. "I wouldn't mind meeting a cowboy someday."

Cassie didn't respond.

"It would be really nice to have someone who shared your interests instead of being like over half the Eagleclaw Trail Riders who leave their husbands at home because they don't like horses."

"Yeah, it does kind of make you wonder, doesn't it?" said Cassie.

"That Dusty is really a nice-looking guy, don't you think?" Terri looked at Cassie sideways.

"I hadn't really given it any thought," Cassie lied.

"Yeah, right, I believe that."

"Why do you say that?"

"Well, I'm not blind. I saw how you guys were looking at each other at the campfire."

Cassie's cheeks burned. "I don't know what you saw, but he's just a professional acquaintance. We are on opposite sides in a current litigation, and I can assure you that we are nothing more than that."

"Okay. Okay. Whatever you say, Cassie. I think I'll go get my horses now. They can eat more in the morning." Terri stood and hurried into the dark, glad to put some distance between herself and Cassie. *Geez, bad day.*

Later that night Cassie tossed and turned in her sleeping bag. She was dreaming about Clem pointing a gun at her and *crack!* The noise sounded like it was right over her tent. Sammy snuggled closer to her. Cassie waited, and the lightning struck again and a second later the thunder boomed.

"Cassie!" Terri called out frantically from her tent next door.

"It's just a thunderstorm. They have them all the time up here."

"Wonderful."

Cassie grabbed her book light and started reading, trying to put her head in a different place than wondering if the lightning was going to sear her tent in half. It only took about an hour, and then a powerful rainstorm began. The sound was deafening as the raindrops pounded against the tent walls and the ground. Cassie finally drifted off to sleep, hoping she wouldn't wind up in a river somewhere.

When she got up the sky was overcast and foggy. The tent had absorbed a lot of water overnight and sagged as she stepped out the door. Terri had put the horses out and a fire was going with a pot of coffee perking.

"Good morning. Coffee's done."

"Great. I didn't sleep much in the thunder and lightning."

"Yeah, me either."

Cassie poured herself a cup of coffee and looked out where the horses grazed in the lush deep mountain grass. A small creek cut through it in a jagged pattern. Flowers splashed the emerald meadow with blue, red, yellow and pink. Even under the dark gray rain-swollen sky, they were a beautiful sight.

Taking a drink of coffee, she turned back to Terri. "We can start breaking down our camp. Looks like it's going to pour again."

"Yeah, it does," Terri said glumly.

"The problem with the rain is that it makes everything just about twice as heavy when it gets soaked. That's the only fly in the ointment, so to speak, in the mountain weather, unpredictable downpours. And then there's snow, too, but we won't even go there now."

Cassie went into her tent, crammed her sleeping bag into the stuff sack, and packed her gear into her bag. She shrugged on her rain slicker and began pulling out her tent poles.

"Don't forget to dry your tent out right away when you get home. I forgot once and it ended up molding."

"Yes, it's brand new, so I was hoping to use it again," said Terri.

They caught their horses in a light rain. Brushing the horses was hard; it was more like just moving the dirt around on their coats. Getting them as clean as she could, Cassie took care to check around the areas where her saddle pad lay and the cinch. Any dirt there would cause a rub on the horse and eventually gall them. They had a long ride out.

Cassie bent to finish tightening her cinch, and water sloshed off the brim of her hat. The rain was beginning to pick up. She threw an extra tarp over her saddle so she'd have a dry seat when she got done.

"Hang on, Murphy. We'll get out of here shortly," Cassie told her patient old packhorse. The bay stood calmly while she threw her sawbuck packsaddle over his back. She cinched it up, taking care to make it tight, but not so tight he couldn't breathe. Once she had the pack on, it would be impossible to tighten without taking everything off and starting over.

She weighed all her gear with her little scale with Terri's help. That was one reason it was nice to have another person along. Otherwise she pretty much would have to go by feel, like the old days. Not that she minded, but it was always nice to make sure your load was even. One person held the load on the little hook of the scale and the other person read the weight.

"Perfect. Thirty-five pounds on this side, too," said Terri.

"Great. We're down a couple pounds on food. Too bad we couldn't have stayed the whole time; we would have been lighter yet," Cassie said, tucking the scale into her saddlebag. "But that just means when we get home we'll start planning our next pack trip!"

Terri laughed. "Hot dog! I can't wait. Hey, I've got my horses done, so when you get finished, would you mind taking a look to make sure I've got it all okay? I'd rather get it right the first time."

"No problem. Just about done here, too." Cassie loaded her tent and foldable chair, laid her mantie over the top, and then tied her double diamond hitch to hold everything together in a nice little package. The double diamond was her favorite because not only did it uniformly hold each side securely in place, but the rope formed a little diamond on each side. The more even the tension, the more uniform the diamond.

Cassie went over to check Terri's load. She had the same basic setup, and she used a smaller horse to pack so it was easier for her to get her gear on.

"So how does Moose look?" Terri asked eagerly. The little white horse had his bags on and the mantie securely tied down.

"Looking good." Cassie checked the load and hitch. "Don't forget to look back from time to time—22 miles is a long way to go."

They mounted up, grabbed their packhorse lead ropes and headed out of the small valley in the drizzling rain.

Chapter Forty-Seven

The rain pitter-pattered on the tent as Dusty opened his eyes. He heard the clank of the hobbles and the pull and munch of the horses. Mike was such a great guy to have along. Having him as a private investigator and a riding partner was the best thing Dusty had ever done, he thought for the umpteenth time. He put his feet in his Romeos, twisted his hat on, threw the tent flap open and stepped out as he shrugged into his rain slicker.

"Well, good morning," greeted Mike.

"It's morning, all right. I don't know about the good. I feel like I've been on a three-day tear. On days like this I can't even remember if I quit drinking, or not."

"Oh, take my word for it, you quit drinking all right."

"Well, then thank God for that, because I sure wouldn't want to feel any worse. How long have the horses been out?"

"It's been about an hour. I was going to just let you get some coffee, and we can hit the trail."

"Well, that was mighty kind of you."

Mike laughed. "I always aim to please."

"Yes, I know you do. The question, of course, would be who?" Dusty joined in the laughter.

It didn't take long to get going. The men had their horses saddled and packhorses highlined in record time. They didn't bother with breakfast and just grabbed some snacks for lunch. They swung into the saddle and rode up the switchbacks over to Crow Lake.

The search and rescue group were gone from Uncle Bob's place when they rode in. The dudes were sitting under a tarp having breakfast. Bob, Andy, and Gold Dust Charlie stood by the cook tent with mugs of coffee in their hands.

"Good morning," called out Dusty. "So what's the plan, Uncle Bob?

"Well, the search and rescue took off at first light. They have got some kind of a grid thing that they go by to systematically search the area. You guys can head over by Ramon Lake and help look."

"Yeah. If nothing else, we should be able to cover more ground quickly."

"And being experienced hunters may help out, too," added Mike.

"We're going to probably just stick around here today and see if the weather blows over. The dudes are interested in doing a little fishing down at the lake, so it looks like it's just going to be a camp day," said Bob.

"And that suits me just fine, too. It's a long ride into this place for an ol' man." Gold Dust smiled.

"Gold Dust, you're no old man. You're just like a horse— you're just getting good!"

"Dusty, you're such a charmer, ain't ya? Nothin' changes there." Gold Dust Charlie laughed and then spit.

The rain gave Dusty a quick chill up the back. "Well, we better hit the trail. It isn't getting any warmer standing around talking." He turned his horse and headed out.

Mike followed Dusty down the trail.Scout trotted along behind, his fur matted from the rain. He jumped a puddle and ran up behind Muley.

The rain didn't let up all morning, and Dusty was glad he had his chinks on. The grass and bushes were full of water, and they sometimes brushed again his legs. The leather chinks covered about three-quarters of his legs over the tops of his boots. They were cooler in the summer than chaps too. His feet remained dry with his tapaderos. He'd learned his lesson a long time ago after getting his feet soaked. The tapaderos covered the front of his stirrups and not only kept his feet dry in the rain, but also kept them warm in the snow.

They were silent for most of the four-hour ride to Ramon. Dusty thought where they might look for Scott's dad and what condition he might be in. He also tried not to think about Cassie and how she was doing post-shooting.

The forest opened with patches of trees occasionally, but nothing that wiped out the view of the ever-present towering peaks around them. Dusty was always in awe, rain or shine, with the beautiful presence of so many mountains. Today with the dark sky and rain, the peaks looked a pale gray. Even the green pine trees were washed out.

They topped a rise and below them lay Ramon Lake. "Well, here we are," said Dusty.

"Looks vacant."

"Yeah, people probably read the weather report before heading out here."

"Maybe, but that doesn't always help."

"You want to sit down for some lunch and then head out of the basin towards Spanish Camp?"

"Sure. A break would probably do the horses good."

They rode to the bottom of the draw by the lake and came to an extinguished campfire area. "Let's tie up here," said Dusty. "There's already logs to sit on. This is probably even where Sally and her family camped."

They tied their horses to a couple of trees. Since they were only stopping for a short time, tying to trees was permitted. Tree savers and highlines were used for longer periods, like overnight, to stop the ground from being dug up and the trees from being ringed.

Dusty threw Scout a dog treat, and they ate some beef jerky and crackers. It felt good to stretch his legs. The rain had let up and the lake was smooth and clear, reflecting the steel sky. Gray clouds swirled around the pinnacles of the peaks above them.

"Well, the good thing about the rain is that the lightning didn't start a fire."

"Yeah, that is the bright side, all right," agreed Mike.

They finished lunch, mounted up, and headed west down the trail. They came up out of the basin and they saw a group of search and rescue people ahead of them.

As they approached on the trail Dusty asked, "Any luck?"

"Unfortunately, yes," said the young man in the front who appeared to be in his 20s. He had dark hair and a sad face. "They found him off the trail about an hour ago. He was curled up in a little ball with no pulse."

"Oh, no." Dusty recoiled in shock.

"We called the Medevac. They should be here shortly."

Dusty felt like he'd been kicked in the stomach. He could only imagine how Sally and Scott were going to feel. He didn't even want to think about it. This is not how backpacking trips were supposed to end. "Is there anything we can do to help?"

"I think we've got it under control. It didn't take very long. He was right below the trail on a rocky drop-off," said the search and rescue person. "I just wish we could have gotten to him sooner. He apparently had a pretty devastating head injury."

Mike just stared hard at the ground, not speaking. He brought his hand up to his cheek and appeared to brush something away.

Dusty swallowed hard. "Well, I guess we'd better head back. Everything appears to be under control here." They all sat mute for a couple long minutes.

The drone of the helicopter broke the silence. "We'll turn the meadow back over to you and get these horses out of here." Dusty reined Muley back the way they'd come.

"Thanks for all your hard work," Mike said in a muffled voice as he rode away.

It was a long quiet ride back to camp.

Chapter Forty-Eight

Dusty and Mike came by Uncle Bob's camp at dusk.

"Any word on it?" he asked, walking up to them.

"Yeah, nothing good. They found him, but the person I talked to said he had no pulse and a devastating head injury. They were airlifting him out."

Bob shook his head. "Well, that's a shame, that's what that is. I'm so sorry for those poor kids."

"Me, too." Mike pushed his hat back and ran a hand over his face.

Dusty pulled his water bottle out of his saddlebag, took a drink, and looked at Bob with a sad face, "It's sure not right that their trip would turn out to be such a disaster."

"You want to step down and join us over here at the fire?"

"No, thanks, Uncle Bob. I think it's been enough of a day. I'd just like to go back to our camp," said Dusty.

"How long you sticking around for?"

"We need to pack up and get out tomorrow. We've got to contact the authorities and make a statement about what happened. Cassie wasn't the only witness."

"Well, I'm sure sorry about this. You boys will have to make it back in for hunting season this year. Ought to be a better time," said Bob as he stroked Muley's nose.

"That sounds pretty good. What do you think, Mike?"

"Well, it's only fair after we had to cut this one short."

"It's a deal then. We'll see you in hunting season."

"So long, Bob. Tell Gold Dust good-bye for us," said Mike.

"Will do, will do. And then you can tell him hello yourself later this fall."

"That sounds like a plan." He and Mike turned their horses and headed past Bob's outfit, waving at the dudes and Charlie in the distance.

The rain had stopped, but the ground was still wet. The creeks they crossed were flowing at a good clip. The sun finally showed itself just as it began to slip behind the mountains. Dusty pulled up for a minute to let his horses drink. *The trip certainly wasn't what I'd planned, but it was an adventure.* He knew now he was going to have to keep an eye out for the two-legged animals as well as the four-legged ones.

He hoped everything had gone all right for Cassie and Terri packing out. Pretty miserable in the rain, but when you're in the mountains, you do what you've got to do. He knew he would be hearing from Cassie, anyway, at least professionally on their case. Maybe he'd even see her riding again, like just two weeks ago at Crystal Mountain. That seemed like such a long time ago. *Never mind. No reason to make my life complicated. I finally just got things simple and I want to enjoy it.*

"Home sweet home," said Mike as they rode into camp.

They unsaddled and put the saddles under the tarps. In no time at all they had a campfire roaring and a coffee pot set on top of their grill on the fire.

"Coffee will be done in a couple of minutes."

"Perfect." Dusty stared into the bright fire with darkness surrounding them. A three-quarter moon had come out, bright enough to illuminate the mountain peaks. The evening sky was midnight blue and the stars twinkled.

Mike gazed at the sky. "Looks like it's going to be a great day for a ride tomorrow."

As they poured themselves a cup of coffee and started talking about their next ride, Ginnie walked into camp.

"Well, there you two are! I was just getting ready to head out tomorrow and wanted to touch base with you." She had on hiking boots, green rain pants and a green slicker. Her hair was pulled back in a ponytail and her cheeks were flushed from hiking.

"Would you like a cup of coffee?" asked Mike, holding up the pot.

"That sounds mighty good right now."

Mike picked up a blue metal cup and handed it to her, the steam pouring off as it hit the cold night air.

"That's a shame about the kids' father." Ginnie wrapped her hands around the cup. "I've been getting a full report on the radio. At least those poor kids are reunited with their mother now."

"Yeah." Dusty couldn't help but feel a stab of pain in his stomach every time he thought about the kids losing their dad.

"Did you hear anything else about what those guys were doing up here, besides causing trouble?" asked Mike.

"That's not conclusive, but the word on the street is that they were running contraband across the border. It's happening a lot more often these days than anyone wants to say." Ginnie took a drink of coffee.

"What kind of contraband?" said Dusty.

"We haven't found that out yet. Whatever it was couldn't have been that heavy to be carried in on those poor horses. I'm sure the Border Patrol and Homeland Security are going to have a lot to talk about with the surviving man."

"Yeah, it's pretty much a lose/lose situation for him." Dusty shook his head and sighed. "He talks, he's probably dead. If he doesn't, they'll probably get him in prison, anyway. Child molesters don't have that long of a shelf life."

"What are your plans now?" asked Ginnie.

"We'll be heading out tomorrow. I'm sure the authorities will want to talk to us. We are witnesses to the abduction and shooting."

"Yeah, I'm heading out myself tomorrow. I need to go to the office and work through the paperwork on this stuff. And then I have to head over to the Sawtooths."

"Are you coming back next summer?" asked Dusty.

"Haven't decided yet. Guess we'll see when the time comes. One thing, though, with

yayhoos like this, I'm going to probably start needing hazard pay!"

They all laughed.

"Yeah, I thought we won the West a long time ago," said Dusty.

"Guess we're going to have to start working on winning it again," agreed Mike.

"Yes. We're going to have to depend on you guys. At this point the Forest Service doesn't allow its employees to carry guns, so it's a good thing I'm fast on my feet."

They all laughed again.

"Well, speaking of that, I better head to bed. I've got a big ride tomorrow." Ginnie put the coffee cup down and stood. "Hope to see you again sometime. Dusty. Your Uncle Bob is really a great guy. I always look forward to dropping into his camp."

"Yes, he is. I'm sure he feels the same way about you, too."

"Pleasure meeting you, Ginnie!" said Mike.

She turned and walked into the night.

The men sat quietly for a few minutes and then Dusty said, "I think Ginnie's got a good point. Long ride in the morning. I'm going to hit the hay."

Dusty left Mike staring into the fire. He turned and headed to his tent, Scout on his heels.

Chapter Forty-Nine

Dusty woke to the familiar smell of canvas tent, the sound of pull, pull, munch and the rattle of hobble chains. He stretched and pulled himself into a sitting position. The campfire crackled. He hoped Mike had the coffee on.

He quickly got dressed in the cold mountain air and went out the already open tent flap—Scout was always an early riser.

Mike sat by the fire, gazing across the lake at the high peaks. The sun was just breaking over the top, a golden glow against the dark blue early morning sky. "Good morning," he said, as Dusty approached.

"What—did you just stay there all night?"

"No. Actually, I did go to bed and get up again since I last saw you."

"Well, you have been a busy guy."

"Guess so," said Mike smiling. "I've been thinking."

"Uh-oh, that's a little scary." Dusty poured himself a cup of coffee and sat down.

"Boy, you just get out of bed all tuned up and ready to go!"

Dusty smiled sheepishly. "I think this clean air keeps me alert."

"Okay, Mr. Alert. Well, I was thinking about our next ride."

"That's one of your finest qualities, Mike, planning the next ride before we get home from the present one."

"Well, maybe because that's the only way I can pack up and leave in good conscience."

"I hear you there. Is this a big ride or a small ride?" asked Dusty, warming to the subject and relaxing.

"Well, they're all big, but we're talking short or long, right?"

"Okay, go on."

"I was thinking about hitting some areas in Oregon."

"Such as?

"Well, I have heard really good things about the Strawberry Wilderness. That's country I wouldn't mind seeing. It's supposed to contain seven different ecosystems."

"Wow, seven different ecosystems in once place," marveled Dusty. "You know, I always wondered—what does that mean?"

"I read it in the book, *Eastern Oregon Horse Pack Trips*, by Dr. Groupe. And to be honest, I don't really know what it means, but it sure sounds cool."

"Yes, it does. So many places to go and so little time to do it."

"Yeah, we may have to ride more and work less."

"Just keep buying those lotto tickets," said Dusty.

Energized by the thoughts of new rides and places to see, Dusty and Mike packed up their camp and as they threw a leg over the saddle, the sun came full into the sky. Flowers were glistening with heavy dew from the rain and the streams were running high. It looked like it was going to be another beautiful day in paradise— the thunderstorm only a distant thought of the past.

Dusty turned Muley, gave him a little kick, and they ascended out of the basin. Scout following on Cheyenne's heels. Mike was a short distance behind, packhorse in tow. The lake shimmered in the early morning sun, clear greenish-blue water. A hawk cried, made a turn over their heads and quickly dropped altitude to its prey.

Dusty breathed it all in. He felt like the world was in perfect order, a peace that he could not put into words. Muley rhythmically moved beneath him, his metal shoes ringing out, striking an occasional stone in the trail. The intoxicating smell of horses and mountains. As Dusty reveled in his good fortune, he looked at the rock formations against a snowy peak. He saw a woman with long light-brown hair on a big gray horse. *What the heck?* He shook his head and took another look—just rocks and snow. Dusty smiled. It could be an omen, and he was thinking it could be a pretty good one. The trail dropped off the arid hillside and Dusty and Mike disappeared into the trees.

Note to Readers

I am passionate about riding and packing horses in the wilderness. My goal in writing this book was to take you on a pack trip. I wanted you to see, feel and smell it. I joined Back Country Horsemen in 1985. The organization is devoted to keeping the backcountry open to horses and mules. I feel like this is becoming a lost sport, and I thought after you spent some time in the saddle you might better understand how valuable the wilderness is to horsemen.

In my next book, **Mountain Cowboys**, Dusty represents a prominent woman in an acrimonious divorce. She is a member of the Eagleclaw Trailriders. After Mike serves the Summons and Petition for Dissolution of marriage, the enraged husband comes to Dusty's office and causes a nasty scene. Dusty and Mike head up to a Back Country Horsemen work party at Buck Creek the following weekend. In the middle of building a bridge on the Ranger Creek trail, in rides Cassie…followed by a tall dark stranger.

Dusty goes to the mountains for peace of mind. On this ride he finds himself fighting for his life…and he has to figure out who is trying to kill him.

Check on my website www.SusieDrougas.com for the release of **Mountain Cowboys**. Sign up on my Newsletter Announce Only and be the first know the release date!

Made in the USA
Middletown, DE
03 March 2015